The Flea Market

The Flea Market

A NOVEL BY

JOHN MOORE

Ekstasis  Editions

National Library of Canada Cataloguing in Publication Data

Moore, John
 The flea market

  ISBN 1-894800-28-1
  I. Title.
PS8576.O6142F53 2003   C813'.54   C2003-910870-8
PR9199.3.O6189F53 2003

Published in 2003 by:
Ekstasis Editions Canada Ltd.
Box 8474, Main Postal Outlet
Victoria, B.C. V8W 3S1

Ekstasis Editions
Box 571
Banff, Alberta ToL oCo

The Flea Market has been published with the assistance of grants
from the Canada Council for the Arts and the Cultural Services
Branch of British Columbia

Printed in Canada

For Joe Ferone,
who said, "It's finished, but it's not over"
and Bill Schermbrucker,
for reminding me I'd failed to save
the damsel in distress...

Addendum from the Debt Control Dept.:
Every author stands in unquantifiable, irreducible debt to almost everyone who has the misfortune to know them, but especially to other writers and publishers who spare the time and energy to read manuscripts, give free editorial advice, generously offer encouragement and pick up the odd bar tab. To Carol Ann Sokoloff and Richard Olafson, I owe eternal thanks for their faith, insight and support. To Bonnie Bowman, Billie Livingston, Jim Christy, Greg Potter and, above all, Peter Trower, I owe a round of cold beers in the holding bar of hell.

The Flea Market

Chapter 1

"I really find a glass of mineral water with ice and lime can be just as satisfying as a vodka and tonic, don't you?"

I came out of the tiny kitchen carrying two translucent green bottles, tall glasses filled with ice, fresh wedges of lime neatly slashed over the rims, on an authentic 1950's Disney-character souvenir TV tray. My ears tingled faintly as I remembered having read that line for the umpteenth time somewhere recently, probably in one of the dozens of fashion magazines stacked beside my bed in a new wicker imitation of an old wicker laundry basket. Laine just might have missed the article among all the others on how to control your boss, cellulite, tummy-bulge, breast droop, social drinking or the premature ejaculations of your current lover, but it wasn't likely.

No, Laine would have scanned it, remembered it and repeated it herself on a more suitable occasion, probably to intimidate some nervous aspiring model or would-be actress whose lunch she was buying as a prelude to the announcement that after careful consideration, The Agency had decided to represent him or her. Taken in one of the more expensive bistros near her office in a reclaimed warehouse space in the old Gastown area of Vancouver, these welcome-to-the-club lunches were actually modest entries on her expense account. Laine never ate more than a handful of assorted designer greens dressed with lemon juice, denying herself even a drop of cold-pressed extra virgin olive oil. The basket of fresh house croutons, fragrant with garlic, was curtly waved away and the disappointed prospective client taught another important lesson *en passant*.

"No garlic during a working day. *Ever*. Not only stays on your breath, but on your fingers, even oozes out your pores. Some of the people you meet in this business may actually be vampires. Why risk offending?"

Laine granted permission to laugh with a marginal smile.

Not a single celebratory sip of wine accompanied these spartan triumphal feasts, only austere mineral waters, another subtle cue that being in the business of selling images of self-indulgence meant joining a secret cult of rigorous abstinence. Clients usually found their own appetites fading anyway as they recalled the way Laine perused their head shots, body shots and resumes with the enthusiasm of a Police Chief pondering the mug shots and rap sheets of violent sexual offenders.

"Yessss… But I wouldn't say no to a slug of gin decently tucked away among the ice cubes to give the bubbles a little flavour."

Laine's drawl was just equivocal enough to let me know she wasn't going to be scathing about having heard it before.

Laine could do that. At forty-two she was head of her own agency representing Vancouver's top models, actors and photographers, the agency west of Toronto which actually dared to call itself simply, The Agency. However demographically small the pond, Laine was the largest frog therein. Though her own looks were just better than average, she was always somehow the most attractive woman in any room, even one window-dressed with her own clients. She could talk sports, politics and investments as intelligently as she talked fashion, art or literature. I always suspected most of the designers, manufacturer's reps, marketing executives, producers and directors she dealt with were secretly fantasizing about Laine as they shoved a sweaty hand up some model's skirt.

Laine had been a designer's rep, managed boutiques, handled personnel in fashion sections of large department chains, worked in makeup and administration for several theatre companies, but never having actually modelled or acted herself, she had none of the reflexes to sit, stand or talk in a conspicuously trained manner the rest of us had drilled into us.

Though I'd been out of modelling for more than five years, I still caught myself standing with my back slightly arched, as if a whippy steel spring had been surgically inserted along the length of my spine, to show off the rags. I knew why I always looked better in jeans and a t-shirt at the laundromat than most women did dressed to the nines in a nightclub. Drunk or sober, I still saw myself walking in full length mirrors with the self-consciously precise grace of the runway. We mockingly called it The Model Toddle, but it would always get you gracefully to the Ladies and enable you to vomit decorously, without getting a speck on your dress or shoes. I still sat with my knees neatly crossed, even when I was alone, an invisible unread book perched atop my expertly dishevelled hair.

"On an untrained body, a drop-dead dress does just that."

Laine said it often enough, but enjoyed being the exception that proved the rule. She could stride down the sidewalk swinging her briefcase like a man or slouch on a couch, swear like a stevedore and still have every man within range fawning over her. I'd been working for her for six months, since my separation from Matthew and return to Vancouver. More than once I'd caught myself deliberately slouching and swearing, smoking with an abandoned wave oblivious of ashtrays, parting my knees to display more than the traditional glimpse of stocking, in imitation of her. As an agent, I was learning more than a new attitude. It was a new set of moves, a new physical vocabulary as well.

"I don't have any gin or vodka, but I might have some brandy left over from dinner the other night. Michael likes cognac."

In fact, I knew for certain there was exactly half a bottle of inexpensive two star cognac in the far corner of the glass-doored kitchen cabinets. The half-bottle had been there, night after night, for weeks. It just wasn't the same half-bottle. There didn't seem to be any way I could explain to Laine why a grown woman with a successful modelling career behind her and a bright future ahead, a woman who had escaped a stifling marriage, who could still turn heads in the trendiest bars, should spend most of her nights sitting up alone watching ancient cable re-runs of Hawaii Five-O until McGarrett finally said, "Book him, Danno. Murder One," drinking brandy and snivelling.

Laine shook her head in approbation

"Brandy and Perrier? Too rough. Like brandy and soda. Something men in safari suits might swill in some explorers' club while they brag about all the animals they've slaughtered. Undrinkable, unthinkable."

Laine didn't want to talk about drinking or about business. She wanted to talk about men. It was a subject, like every other, on which she had definite opinions. All Laine's men were between twenty-five and thirty-two years old.

"Under twenty-five, they're too young to train. Like puppies. No attention span. They can't resist any little bitch who wags her tail at them. And, of course, they're still into that rugby scrum male-bonding thing where their idea of an evening on the town is to drink too much beer with their buddies and watch moronic girls with silicone tits take off very improbable lingerie to deafening rock music, then come home and throw up. If one makes it to twenty-five without turning into a baseball-capped walking life-support system for a major brewery, he can be taken in hand… By a woman who's mature enough to know what she wants, of course. If they're ever going to learn how to make a woman happy, and to be happy doing it, of course, that's the time…"

Like all assertive people, Laine said "of course" a lot. It made people disinclined to disagree with her. The implication was that if you didn't see her point you must be impossibly dense or irretrievably out of it, babe. It was another of Laine's mannerisms I'd caught myself aping lately. Sometimes in the office, interviewing a client or trying to sell one on the phone, I was shocked, like an eavesdropper, at the brittle patronizing sound of my own voice. Trouble was, it worked. Just as the tricks of makeup and modelling could turn a fairly ordinary looking girl into a babe that had men crunching each other like a football scrimmage just to be close to her, I found people deferring to me almost as readily as they did to Laine.

Laine was right about men, too. At least within the terms of her own definition. Laine's men were always handsome, always had the cutting-edge haircut, clothes designed to look inexpensive to all but the untrained eye, always smelled of a subtle *au courant* cologne. They were never gay, though many of them were the envy of every queer she knew or dealt with. Laine knew a lot of gay men, but she didn't believe in trying to convert them.

"Never pinch hit with two out in the bottom of the ninth, baby."

Laine's men were expected to talk sports, politics, art and money as astutely as she did. Masculine, but never over-bearing, charming to her friends, sincerely polite to her guests and clients, they lived in quiet but constant attendance on her, opening doors, lighting her cigarettes, removing or replacing her coat, remembering her bag, briefcase and social engagements. All these tasks had to be performed with discreet devotion but never allowed to appear slavish.

Her relationships weren't as one-sided as they seemed. Laine's young men got as well as they gave. Not just gifts of elegant jewellery, suits and shirts that lay temporarily beyond their economic reach. These trinkets they were expected to reciprocate as their taste and financial status improved under her tutelage. By far the most valuable gift they received from Laine was direction.

Cynical young copywriters dreaming the great novel would find themselves aggressively jockeying for and achieving coveted promotions as creative directors of ad agencies.

Photographers with inclinations toward social realism would simply be so swamped with fashion assignments through her network of contacts they'd have to move to prestigious loft studios further from their East End friends and nearer Laine's Gastown nerve centre. Youthful left-wing documentary film-makers found themselves suddenly in demand to direct rock music videos and commercials in which struggling musicians and actors, many of them represented by The Agency, made their debuts. Starving young painters were invited to mount one-man shows at fashionable South Granville Street galleries which sold out on opening night. Vague surrealist poets were offered editorial positions on the staffs of trendy fanzines or trade magazines. Laine's rolodex was known as Pandora's Box, but only late at night, when the party was winding down and everyone had already had enough to drink or inhale they could pretend to remember nothing in the morning.

Taking a sip of her Perrier, Laine kicked off her maroon Bally flats. They hit the uncarpeted hardwood floor with two sharp echoing raps. You seldom had to wait for the other shoe to drop with Laine.

"The trouble starts when they turn thirty-five. That's when they find the first gray hair in the sideburns. That's when the male stomach muscles lose their natural tone and they have to start doing a hundred abdominal crunches every day. That's when the nineteen-year-old bubblehead blondes start looking cute again."

I nipped at my own Perrier without replying. I'd heard the Discourse on Men before. I knew Guy, Laine's current beau, was thirty-two and holding. He'd been an apprentice goldsmith, of all things, when Laine met him. Now he designed minimalist jewelry at his own chic Granville Island boutique. Laine abruptly changed the subject.

"Have you heard from Matthew?"

I shrugged ambivalently.

"I've heard from his lawyer. He sent me a separation agreement to sign."

So like Matthew. As a writer, he always hoarded his words for the millions of anonymous strangers he believed would read them one day. He talked more in the beginning, when my modelling supported us both while he wrote, but after his first novel was published and acclaimed and we moved from Vancouver to Toronto, he seemed to speak less as he wrote more. I occupied myself with our small house off St. Clair West, renovating and decorating, turning it into a venue for gatherings of writers, critics, agents and publishers I imagined sitting around my table. My fantasy salon. Matthew spent more and more time at his trestle bench in the low basement where the glare of an old gooseneck lamp threw spooky shadows among the cobwebbed heating ducts.

He wouldn't let me clean the basement out, let alone have it finished and painted. There were still boxes and bags of junk left by the previous owners down there in a corner. One muggy summer night, when I pursued him to his lair, we made a game of going through that alien trash, trying to match up pieces of torn photos and letters, uncrumpling old yellowed bills and invoices, holding up the stale smelling clothes, reinventing the lives of the mysterious antecedents at our address. Then we made love as violently as strangers on the cool cement.

"What does he want?"

I shrugged again.

"Everything, more or less. I think I might just sign it and

send it back. I don't want anything except not to have to fight anymore. Or not to have to talk to someone who fights by not talking back, except to state facts in a way that is so flat it's hateful. It's almost funny, you know? There's so much pain and tears in the destruction of a marriage, but that's not what ends it. That's not what kills your feelings finally. It's exhaustion. You just get too tired to fight anymore and all you can do is leave."

Laine slammed her glass down on the smiling face of Minnie Mouse.

"Bullshit. You take that agreement straight to your lawyer and have it re-written."

"I don't have a lawyer. I don't think I want one."

Laine's no-nonsense Agency business voice cut me off.

"This is what lawyers are for. They're goons in suits. You pay them to legally beat the shit out of people you don't have time or energy to waste on, people who just want to drag you down to their level and fuck your life over because they have nothing better to do and their whole lives to do it. Bring it into the office Monday and I'll have my lawyer go over it and tell you what to do."

The last thing I wanted right then was someone else to tell me what to do. I'd had fifteen years of that from Matthew, months of it from David, the lover I took in a desperate bid to get Matthew's attention, not to mention the shit-storm of supportive input from girlfriends, my family, my doctor, a marriage counsellor and a psychiatrist. Laine waved her arm at the apartment living room, empty but for the two folding director's chairs we occupied and a low wooden tea chest I hadn't found time to refinish which supported the tray, Perrier bottles and her own perfectly pedicured feet.

"I mean, look at this place, Eve… You have this beautiful apartment and not a stick to call your own. You don't just walk away from a marriage with nothing but the clothes in your walk-in. You're lucky you don't need a pot to piss in or you'd have nothing to cook with. You'd feel much more settled in your mind if you'd settle in here and create your own space. Something that's you and you alone."

I nodded wearily.

"I know. It's a lovely place. It's just almost too perfect, you know?"

I'd been lucky to sublet the apartment, through Laine, from a model who was trying her wings in Toronto in exchange for names and numbers Laine and I could provide. The model sublet from a choreographer who was kicking up his heels in New York. Just inside the invisible frontier of Kitsilano, it was one of the rare older buildings whose hardwood floors, moldings and stained glass had been restored rather than demolished to make way for a towering warren of minuscule bachelor cells.

"I know it needs just the right things. Not just any old things and I don't want any of my things from Toronto to, well, remind me… You know?"

Laine patted my shoulder comfortingly as she looked around at the bare walls of the unfurnished room.

"Of course, I know. You have a whole new life and your beautiful new space should reflect that. Everything in it should be a personal statement, right down to the shelf-paper… I know! We'll go around to the flea markets on Sunday! Just the two of us! You won't believe your eyes. The most marvellously tacky things. Plant-holders shaped like panthers. Statues of Venus with clocks in their stomachs. And the furniture!

18

Really, you'll get some wonderful ideas. The best ones are out in Surrey, of course." She spoke of the place with the enthusiasm Anglo-Irish aristocrats once used to describe anything Beyond The Pale. "But it'll be fun! We'll make a day of it!"

"Oh, I wouldn't want to spoil your day with Guy."

Sunday was Laine's day with her lover, given over to long brunches in bed or sunny cafes, *sans* cell-phone, to walking and talking and reading the *New York Times Review of Books* and the *Los Angeles Times,* watching videos of classic films while grazing on organic popcorn. The week belonged to The Agency and Saturday to her fourteen-year-old daughter Lisa, the issue of Laine's own brief marriage to an advertising executive which lasted just long enough to produce a female child who was deaf. Since the divorce, Lisa had lived with Laine's mother in Burnaby. Saturday also often involved shows, openings, launches which Lisa attended with Laine instead of hanging out at the mall with her friends. When Lisa hung out at the mall, it was with her mother and a platinum Visa card.

I was uncomfortable around Lisa. I told myself it was her deafness, which gave the girl an uncanny stillness from which she seemed to project silence into the noisiest room, but I knew it was more than that. Lisa was about to be beautiful. The growth spurt that had made her tall and slim had not been allowed to make her gangly and clumsy. Laine had seen to that. The Agency's top models had trained Lisa to walk, stand and sit with precocious poise.

Laine was staring at the lime floating in her Perrier like a corpse in a swimming pool.

"On second thought, I will have a shot of that cognac. Straight."

I quickly produced two snifters with generous amber

puddles of brandy caught in the bottoms like stagnant water over clogged drains. Laine took a huge swallow of hers and shuddered.

"Did I say something? Is there something wrong between you and Guy?"

Laine took another deep swig of brandy and chewed fiercely on the filter of her slim 100 millimetre cigarette.

"Not any more. Not since I found out he's been playing hide-the-hotdog with some twenty-year-old cunt of an exotic dancer who commissioned a clit-ring from him. A stripper! I mean, what the fuck is that about?"

I took a big burning gulp of my own brandy and stared politely at the big blank beautiful wall across the room.

Chapter 2

As planned, the following Sunday we set out in Laine's glossy black Porsche 911S. With a wave of a 7 a.m. cigarette Laine dismissed my observation that the coupe had even less room to transport anything we might buy than the back seat of my antique Austin Mini. Besides, Laine pointed out, she knew the way. She said it the way someone might say they 'knew the way' to the headwaters of the Amazon. We were only going to Cloverdale but I knew Laine would rather drive than be driven, even in a limo.

The minimalist interior of the Porsche, its few gauges functional rather than decorative, looked like the cockpit of an old fighter plane and Laine drove like she was in a dog-fight. Swooping in and out of lanes as we made our way across the city, she cut off other drivers with an erect finger raised in response to the angry blasts of their horns. We merged with the freeway traffic on the Trans-Canada at a fearless velocity.

"Why a Porsche? Why not a convertible Beamer or even a Mercedes?"

As I said it I realized I already knew the answer. Porsches are the severely Teutonic car male lawyers, doctors, brokers and film producers buy themselves to signal ruthless efficiency as much as to celebrate their success. You seldom see a woman behind the wheel of one. I was surprised when Laine admitted as much, but her explanation wasn't as simple as I'd expected.

"A few years ago, I took a trip up to Kelowna with a very rich young Arabian guy who wanted to get into film production. We drove up in his new Porsche Targa to visit some relatives of his. As both an older woman and an infidel I didn't expect to be a big hit with the family, but I thought as least we'd have some fun with that sleek hundred thousand dollar beast on the Coquihalla. All the way up, he drove like a perfect gentleman, meaning he didn't drive at all. Never broke the speed limit by a single kay-pee-aitch. On the way back I kept waiting for him to finally let that car off the leash, to start *driving*. Then it dawned on me that he was *terrified*. Really afraid of all that power in his hands. He didn't deserve that car. He could *afford* it, that was all."

I vaguely recalled references to The Sheik in Laine's long distance phone calls.

"Whatever happened to him?"

Laine shrugged.

"How should I know? Probably married to some fat Persian cunt who wears a full burka to bed and cranks out kids like sausages. Halfway home, we stopped to stretch our legs and I asked him if I could try driving his beautiful car." She batted her eyes like she was auditioning for a remake of the

Valentino silent classic. "Girl, I blew the doors off everything that got in our way between Hope and Vancouver and probably sucked enough lug-nuts off the eighteen wheelers to wobble them into jack-knife crashes. When I handed him the keys, I had to help him out of the car. Swarthy men don't actually turn white with fear, you know? They go a kind of chalky taupe. Very unappealing. He didn't know anything about film, anyway. He just had too much money and no idea what to do with it."

I was glad I wasn't driving. I loved my old Mini, a souvenir from my bachelorette days. My brother inherited it when I got married, carefully maintained and reluctantly returned it after the separation. Laine said the Mini was 'retro cute' and just the thing for a working girl in the city. It would run forever on a shooter of gas and you could park it in your evening bag. Still, on the few occasions she'd ridden in it, she'd remarked that it had less 'poop' than her Cuisinart and I sensed Laine thought I drove like an old lady. She fidgeted in the Mini. She couldn't stretch her long legs. Worst of all, she wasn't driving.

Reclining my seat an inch, I closed my eyes as Laine slipped the Porsche neatly under the nose of a tanker truck, outran a family station wagon full of kids and cut off a Corvette before pulling over into the now empty right lane. She dropped the car into fifth gear and lit one of her long cigarettes from the dash lighter in one motion.

"Did you see Michael last night?"

Reluctantly, I opened my eyes just enough to indicate attention. Laine's question reminded me of the dull ache along my inner thighs, the pleasantly bruised feeling on the keystone of bone between. Yes, I'd 'seen' Michael the night before. Laine eyed a gold 70's Trans-Am making tentative advances in the driver's side mirror. Almost imperceptibly, the Porsche snugged down on its shocks as our speed increased.

"Of course, he's told you all about Amanda…"

I nodded. Yes, he'd told me all about Amanda and her two lovely children by Chris Newman, a photographer who regularly worked at The Agency. Michael often worked with Chris and they'd become close friends. Michael's dark, mature good looks kept him in demand, advertising everything from cologne to cashmere sweaters, from single malt whisky to fishing tackle and Jaguars. Michael loved doing Jag ads in a tux. One of my old friends, who wasn't in the business where beauty is a given, took ten minutes to recover the power of speech after being introduced to Michael at a party. She finally managed a breathless whisper in the kitchen.

"My God! He looks like James Bond!"

I crossed my legs. A flush, like prickly heat, rose toward my navel, surrounding it like an island in a typhoon. Michael made love like the legendary spy, nothing kinky, but as straight, hard and insatiable as they came, so to speak. He also left like a spy, without waking me. And there was no denying he did tend to go on about Amanda lately. Her talent, her patience, not to mention her charming children. Laine swept threateningly close to a lumbering Winnebago, passing it like it was still hooked up to the holding tank flusher, without bothering to signal.

"He's going to marry her, of course." A stream of smoke from her nostrils was instantly sucked away by the interior ventilation. "The way he talks about her… My God, the poor bastard. Sweet, long-suffering Amanda is going to clip two birds with one shot of her thirty-eight C magnums. She's not only going to nail a man who'll spend the rest of his life trying to make it up to her for Chris going AWOL, but the man is one of Chris' best friends. *There's* a girl who really knows how to turn the cold tossed salad of revenge into the full meal deal…"

Admiration and approbation were mixed in her voice like a perfect cocktail. I nodded, agreeing because it seemed easier than arguing about something I hadn't allowed myself to think about. Of course, Laine was probably right and she was only warning me for my own good. She'd known Chris, Amanda and Michael during the years I was in Toronto. At one time or another, she'd represented them all and, for awhile, before Amanda quit acting to marry Chris, all three at once. Chris had been one of Laine's young men and before that, an old friend of Matthew's and mine. We introduced them. They parted, amicably enough, not long after his thirtieth birthday bash held in the recently renovated Yaletown loft commensurate with his success. At the party, he'd shown more than a polite interest in Amanda, three years his senior. Laine glanced confidentially at me, keeping one eye on the fast flow of traffic.

"I warned them both, of course. For marriage, a woman still needs an older man. Someone established in his own right, secure enough to be patient and supportive of her career. Someone who can afford to be indulgent. But Amanda wouldn't listen to me. All she could hear was the ticking of her bloody biological clock… Poor Chris. He actually thought I was jealous. Can you imagine? I mean, she's not *that* much younger than I am, but he thought he was being so *mature,* trying to outgrow this relationship with an older woman. He suddenly realized it was all very Freudian and incestuous, if you can believe that…"

She giggled suggestively. "Of course, I pointed out if that was true, he'd have gone out and found himself a teenage queen with good genes and an IQ in the double numbers, not some stage-struck neurotic it would be positively a compliment to call a has-been. As an actress, Amanda simply never was. A few years at RADA gave her nothing but that silly patronizing Trans-Atlantic accent Canadians affect when they live in Britain for a few months and acquire a few amusing stories about Oliver Reed getting blind drunk and wrecking London pubs. Her best role was the melodrama she did about how she was giving up her career, her life in the *theatah*, *dahling*, to be Chris' mate and bear his young, blah, blah. A shtick she's still playing for all it's worth, if Michael's dialogue is anything to go by…"

Laine snubbed her cigarette and lit another, snaking through slower traffic with one hand on the wheel. I watched the shifting cars ahead for the flashed tail-light of a suddenly applied brake or the late signal of an impromptu lane change that would be the last thing I saw. My fingers dangled, brushing the countersunk doorhandle. It would happen in slow-motion, the way accidents always seem to the participants, but I would magically be able to move at normal speed, fling the door open and throw myself free, toward the grassy boulevard, before the shattering impact.

I'd die, because no one could survive such a tumble at this speed, but I would die beautifully and painlessly, my neck delicately broken. Policemen, paramedics and the cortege of ghouls who always slow down to cop a peek at an accident would be stunned into silent shame and mourning by my tragic beauty in death. Having remained in her precious Porsche, Laine would be an unidentifiable smear of charred blood and offal across the smashed glass and frozen gauges of the twisted dashboard. They'd have to bury her in the car.

I lit one of my own cigarettes, the short Camel Plains living with Matthew had addicted me to, making an effort to keep my hand steady. I knew my silence was irritating Laine, whose life was entirely verbal—meetings, negotiations, discussions, arguments, phone calls, gossip. It drove her to rant on, filling up the silence with words. Silence was the only defense against Laine. Ironically, I realized it was the very same weapon Matthew used so often against me.

"Of course, I had to keep a straight face. I mean, when he takes it so seriously... After all she gave up for him!" She parodied Michael's own slight trace of a faux-British accent expertly, reminding me of yet another thing he and Amanda had in common. "But really, it's all I can do not to laugh in his face sometimes. I have to run off to the girls room so often to giggle, I'm sure he thinks I've got a weak bladder..."

I smiled quietly to myself. If you were going to fantasize, you might as well be Cecil B. about it. Thrown free of the wreck, I'd miraculously survive, having hit my head just hard enough to give me the total amnesia beloved of soap-opera writers. A Highway Patrolman, a truck driver, or some young man running away from an unspecified tragedy of his own, would find me lying in the grass while Laine barbecued in the burning Porsche in the slightly out of focus background. Smitten by my beauty, he would wrap me in his jacket and carry me off into another life, blessing the luck that had given him this chance to start his own anew with a beautiful stranger. He would care for me and patiently teach me to live again, to speak and dress myself and eat with a knife and fork and he would adore me. I would love him for his kindness and because no memory or thought of any other life would occur to me.

There would be headlines. *Mysterious Model Disappearance Unsolved. Police Have No Clues.* They would remove Laine's remains from the dash with a squeegee but find no trace of me. There would be pictures—grainy party ensemble snaps taken by gossip columnists, accompanied by my own best head shots captioned, *Have You Seen This Woman?*—in all the papers. Matthew would abandon his latest novel, fly out from Toronto, badger the police, offer rewards, hire private investigators, finally pursue the search alone, a man obsessed.

He would find me eventually. I wouldn't recognize him, but politely serve him coffee and cake before I went out into the yard to soothe the skinned knee of one of the angelic children I'd borne to my rescuer. He and Matthew would look at each other, *the way men do*, without speaking. Then Matthew would go away without saying goodbye, catching a last glimpse of me from the street while I returned his gaze with kindly but vacant eyes.

Not Booker Prize material maybe, but not so much worse than some of the shit Matthew had written since he'd become famous and every sycophant magazine editor wanted his name on their covers. Laine swerved left to avoid traffic merging from the New Westminister on-ramps.

"Her divorce will be final any day now, so don't be surprised if he seems rather preoccupied and 'busy' all the time. I imagine she'll really start turning the screws once she's got that Decree Absolute in her hot little hands like a script from Francis Ford Coppola…"

I sighed a stream of smoke, steeling myself to the idea. After all, I'd told myself from the beginning Michael was to be *fun*, that was all. After David—an old boyfriend who'd taken advantage of my brief solo visit with my parents in Vancouver in the midst of our marital crisis to declare his undying love over a Starbucks latte, which escalated like a tribal war into a candlelit dinner of spaghetti puttanesca and then to full-on Biblical adultery—I was entitled to some fun. David turned out to be no fun at all, much less the love of my life.

I should have reminded myself how our brief high school courtship ended. During our three dates, which consisted of meeting at North Van Community Centre teen dances, David acted like the perfect gentleman while all my girlfriends squealed, "Oooh, he looks just like George Harrison!" After the third, he escorted me up the darkened front stairs of my parents house as usual, but when I turned to indulge in the now obligatory fifteen minute tonsil-probe and tit-grope we called the Goodnight Kiss, I discovered he had dropped his jeans to his knees.

Apparently I was to extend the Goodnight Kiss to the object which looked like a blind shrew trapped in a Brillo pad. My knees went weak, but instead of falling to them as expected, I burst out laughing, opened the door and shut it firmly behind me, leaving him with his passion cooling in the night air. Inside, I collapsed in such hysterical giggles my parents naturally assumed I'd been smoking dope.

Everyone thought I'd left Matthew for David, no matter how vehemently I insisted he was only a supportive friend, helping me through a difficult time. That wasn't strictly true, I had to admit when I was alone with a brandy, imagining myself being questioned by Steve McGarrett. David was still what magazines call 'ruggedly handsome,' his longish hair and *bandito* moustache reminiscent of our high school days. He'd become an independent contractor, lean and bronzed by the sun, a non-smoking Marlboro man who'd been setting panties aflutter for so long it was a reflex.

We enjoyed a few months of illicit bliss, lolling in the hot-tub on his property overlooking Indian Arm, surrounded by scented candles and wine and The Eagles on his massive stereo, complicated by the indignant gossip of most of the friends Matthew and I shared in Vancouver. A few refused to take sides in the marital war, like Jack Morrison, a writer who lacked Matthew's talent for self-promotion, though Matthew grudgingly admired his talent, and Harry Lamb, a musician who'd inherited some kind of title and land back in England and spent a lot of his time there.

But even Jack and Harry were united in their loathing of David, who they'd gone through high school with, a few years ahead of me. They weren't just the older guys in school, they were the cool guys, major players and they all hung out together, which made it hard for a junior high new girl with noticeable breasts and a cute face to read the internal rivalries, mostly sexual, hidden in the fine print. It's occurred to me since that I was never anything more than a trophy fuck for any of these assholes, including the one I married. David couldn't get me to suck it, much less spread, but Matthew did and David never forgave or forgot. He waited and watched and finally got even with both of us by getting me to suck and fuck him after I was married to Matthew. For awhile, my favourite sexual fantasy has involved binding Matthew and David's cocks and balls tightly with a piano wire as they stand face-to-face and lighting a bonfire fire between their feet, then masturbating while taking bets on which one will run from the flames and emasculate himself first.

David's on-and-off girlfriend, Carolyn, got wind of our affair in San Francisco, where she was studying film set design. Carolyn, who'd dumped him for the umpteenth time after fucking a couple of his best friends as a valedictory gesture, suddenly discovered a desperate need for something she didn't want as long as nobody else did. Within a week of knowing about us, she was back. A month later, she was carrying David's child. Within two months, everyone who knew us, knew it. It was an old trick, lowest and dirtiest of them all, but like most things tried and true, it worked. David agonized, but I'd seen the writing on the bathroom mirror in Carolyn's distinctively tacky lipstick: *WE'RE PREGNANT*!!!

David had neglected or forgotten to wipe it off before I came for dinner the night he dropped that *bombe* for dessert. I'm still not sure how I could be so smitten with a man over an *aperitif* and feel nothing but pity as I consigned him to his chosen Hell over dessert. I'd been living in the mirror myself, I realized while savouring the game hens stuffed with wild rice. The thing growing in Carolyn's belly was a fact. Not some homunculus procured by a witch, but a human being in whose creation David had taken an active, if unwitting, part. It was, I decided as I polished off the mango ice cream mousse, his fucking problem.

Oh, there was a moment, while we lingered over liqueurs and he marvelled at my understanding, my compassionate womanly wisdom, when I counted back the days to my last period, calculated the odds on really giving him something to agonize about, and considered whispering that I wanted him to take me now, one last time, right there on the table amid the leftover mousse and never mind the condom because I really needed to feel as close to him as possible.

Instead, I extricated myself from his damply passionate, speculative how-about-one-for-the-road embrace and drove home, parked the Mini, model-toddled down the hall, locked the door of my perfect empty apartment behind me and drank a tumbler full of brandy in one long swallow before I threw up a bellyful of oaked chardonnay, bruschetta, wild rice stuffing, roast game hen, mango mousse and no longer flaming Sambuca.

Michael was supposed to be the antidote. With his perfect looks and perfect manners, his knowledge of fine wines and antique prints and classic cars, he was to have been the cure for the feelings I got when some of my former friends I now called The Cunts phoned from Toronto to tell me what an outgoing bachelor my literary hermit husband had become since I left. Even Laine had heard rumours and questioned me. I'd rehearsed my reply, just the right amount of indifference and concern, leavened with genuine regret.

"I hear he's doing some entertaining and hitting the clubs a bit. I'm happy for him. I'm glad he's coming out of his shell. I'm just sorry it took my leaving him to make him start doing things I'd been trying to get him to do for years…"

One thing bothered me, though, I admitted to Laine alone.

"I know it sounds stupid, but what bugs me is the thought of these people sitting on my furniture in the house I decorated and using my things when I'm not there. You know?"

Of course, Laine understood. Guests at her Kitsilano townhouse were politely discouraged from handling her possessions or tinkering with her sensitive state-of-the-art appliances, each of which had been fine-tuned for optimum performance. Offers to help with the dishes were declined with a disquisition on the proper care of true bone china, which had to be washed in the gentlest detergents, one piece at a time, in a sink lined with tea towels to cushion the fragile rims against chips and cracks.

"It's not far now."

We hurtled down a long straight flat road off the freeway interchange, past muddy green fields with fences that went unchallenged by tableaux of contented black and white cows.

Chapter 3

Laine was directed to a spot in the large mostly vacant parking lot by a bored teenage boy in yellow rain gear that seemed prophetic. There had been spatters of summer rain in the city during the night. I remembered half-waking to the comforting whisper of the drizzle on the laurel hedges in the alley, the metronomic dripping of the eaves, the even more comforting pressure of Michael's chest against my back. Aware he was awake, aroused and had probably woken me with a deliberate caress, I started to turn to him but he held me still on my side, drew up my legs and gently entered me. I didn't come, didn't even want to, content to glissade back down into the soft black canyon of sleep as I felt him tense, glaze my backside with a teaspoon of jism, then sigh gratefully and kiss the back of my neck.

Later I woke again to burrow into the warm rift his body had left in the sheets and inhale the faint expensive scent of his after-shave from the pillow. I opened my eyes just in time to hear the entry door click shut and lock as he let himself out. When I finally got up it was a brilliant day, the sun glaring off rain-polished leaves and paintwork. The smell of fresh coffee drifted from the automatic maker I'd presumptuously filled for two and set the night before. The sound of my favourite songs being referred to as 'classic rock' by a patronizing dee-jay blared from the clock-radio. Despite a bruisingly hot shower, an hour of too much coffee too early in the morning left me feeling edgy and exhausted before Laine arrived.

"You have to get there early for the bargains. Otherwise everything is picked over."

How could you worry about a lot of second, third, fourth or fifth-hand things being *picked over?* I let it pass. Now in the Fraser Valley, we caught up with the clouds. It was warm, but the sun failed to break through and the low ceiling was under-lined with black in places, like mascara slightly smeared with tears. Rain hung over our heads like an unspoken threat. Laine stepped around a large puddle to spare her immaculate Reeboks.

"It might not be that good here today. Usually most of the good stuff is outside, but a lot of people probably think it's going to rain."

From the look of the glowering sky, a lot of people were probably right. I followed Laine through the main gate of a chain link fence guarded by a jerry-built blue sentry box that looked like a portable toilet heisted from a construction site. A fat woman wearing a faded Tommy Hilfiger sweatshirt too small for her and a dirty canvas change apron took a dollar coin from Laine, who paid the fifty cents admission for us both.

I wasn't as quick as Laine, who'd been through this before and snatched her hand away from the ink-stamp. Before I could react, I found myself staring down at a splotch of indelible ink, like a Rorsach blot or sloppy jailhouse tattoo, on the back of my wrist left by the cylinder stamp concealed in the woman's pudgy hand.

"*You* can go out and come back in." Her tone implied a privilege that would be denied my fussy, probably snooty friend unless she forked out another half-buck.

"Thank you."

I said it automatically as I contemplated my defaced skin, wondering why for the umpteenth time in my life I was thanking somebody for something I didn't want. A few steps inside the gate, I surreptitiously licked a finger and tried to rub off the stamp. Spit and friction made no discernable difference to the indecipherable blotch and I gave up, suddenly reminded of teen dances at the Community Centre I went to with both Matthew and David. Having your hand stamped then was more than just a passport to slip out to the parking lot for a few swigs of illicit lemon gin, a few tokes on a joint passed in a car with the windows rolled up or fifteen minutes of frantic squirming with a boy's probing hand sandwiched between skintight jeans and moist yearning flesh. It was a badge of status, a sign that you had *been there*, a brand of belonging you brandished brazenly, mourned and hurried to renew when it finally faded.

A big black crossbreed dog ran past me, pursued by a short man in trousers too narrow for his wide wobbling buttocks and too long for his stubby legs. Cornered against a parked van from which boxes of unidentifiable goods were being unloaded, the dog turned and snarled. Cursing in an

unrecognizable language, the man beat the dog mercilessly
with a short length of chain swung from his right hand until
the dog flattened itself on the broken pavement and whim-
pered. I winced at the blows, as if they were falling on my own
flesh, and looked away. Snapping the chain around the cowed
dog's neck, the man dragged the cringing animal back past me
in the direction they'd come from, still sputtering untranslat-
able curses. Unable to find Laine in the crowd milling around
the improvised midway of trucks and vans, each with a tarp or
plastic awning, I felt like a little girl lost on some dismal fair-
ground, about to cry.

At last, I spotted her waving from a nearby table covered
with a pile of old shoes. She pointed to a pair of evidently
unworn cowboy boots in heavily tooled bright red leather.

"Wouldn't you just love to buy these for Michael?"

I smiled hesitantly, trying to fall in with her determined-
ly upbeat "Isn't this fun?" mode, which followed so unexpectedly after the unrelieved bitchiness of the car ride. Dutifully, I
looked at the boots. Michael might wear them once, as a joke,
to a party or club, but he had a closet filled with Gucci moc-
casins, Bally loafers, British-made oxfords and brogues, dress
boots from Florshiem and John Fleuvog. I couldn't see these
garish cast-offs finding a permanent place in his wardrobe.
Inevitably, they would be thrown into a box in the course of
some spring cleaning or apartment change, perhaps when he
moved in with Amanda, and consigned to the Salvation Army
or Mental Health charity pickup. I glimpsed a possible future;
Laine and I, months or years from now, going to a flea market
or swap meet and finding this same pair of red boots on one
of the tables, sad as a wedding-gift recognized in a pawnshop
window.

There was no way I was going to buy them, even as a joke, but I was spared having to explain the vague poignancy that inspired my decision. Laine had already moved on to the next table to rummage through boxes of eight-track tapes and vinyl records from the Sixties and Seventies. Stacks and stacks of albums by The Moody Blues, Deep Purple, Neil Diamond, The Village People, Boney M, the Electric Light Orchestra, The Eagles, and hundreds of groups recalled only by the jacket blurb "Includes the Hit Single!" flicked into the light for a moment like files searched by a coroner's secretary.

Under the flimsy protection of a droopy awning, two men were arguing loudly nearby.

"I can't take less than twenty-five…"

"I'll give you twenty for the lot…"

"I paid twenty."

"If you paid twenty, you wouldn't be here. I'll give you twenty. Cash."

"No deal. I gotta get twenty-five…"

"I bought from you before. You bought from me. Here's twenty-two and you owe me a favour."

"A favour? I could get fifty, maybe seventy-five, downtown. I'm doin' you a favour at twenty-five to save myself the drive and the aggravation!"

"Twenty-two fifty is all I'll go. You can get fifty or more downtown? What the fuck're you doin' here?"

"I'll get fifty."

"You'll get thirty, spend ten bucks on gas, get a flat tire and a parking ticket."

"I'll get fifty, no problem."

"You'll get fucked."

"Not by you for a lousy twenty."

"I said twenty-two fifty, didn't I?"

A small crowd gathered to watch the haggling. One of the principals, feigning indifference to the outcome, suddenly turned his attention to the onlookers. I pretended to be interested in a large power tool whose purpose I couldn't imagine, hoping to be ignored. It was a mistake. He interpreted it as the faint scent of a sale.

"Only fifteen bucks. You'd pay fifty, downtown. One of the handgrips is missing."

I nodded as though I'd been about to mention the deficiency myself.

"I think my husband already has one of these."

I faded back into the crowd. Matthew probably did have one of whatever it was. He used tools fastidiously and always returned them to their metal boxes, so like coffins, or to the wall hooks above the workbench in the vine-covered garage behind the house in Toronto. No doubt he acquired the habit of neatness and precision from using his father's tools as he grew up. I remembered the tidy workshop in his parents' basement, next to the low-ceilinged rec room where we used to fuck furtively on an old leather couch while his Mom and Dad watched TV directly over our heads. What with Matthew's panting punctuated by bursts of sitcom canned laughter, the clammy grip of leather on my ass, the bound feeling at my ankles due to the knot of jeans and panties I lowered but refused to actually take off, plus the crick I always got in my neck from twisting my head around to watch over his heaving shoulder for a foot coming down on the top stair, my orgasms were infrequent.

Like the workshop, Matthew's study at the Toronto house was as neat as a surgical theatre. A wide-topped teacher's desk I'd found in a junk store and refinished as a birthday present faced the large window and the view of the cemetery beyond. From the second floor, you couldn't really see a lot of headstones or graves, only the high stone wall and the branches of the trees with their ever-changing leaves. It wasn't a depressing view, if you didn't brood on it. Certainly not as depressing as looking out of a highrise catacomb in downtown Toronto at a wall of identical highrise catacombs across the street. Two antique wooden filing cabinets with modern fireproof inserts contained Matthew's files and drafts of works in progress, along with his precious original manuscripts. Shelves Matthew built himself, indulging in expensive black walnut, lined the walls. They held typescripts and galleys of his own works, painstakingly bound, boxed and indexed by me, as well as proof copies and first editions of his own books and those of writers he'd met, each suitably inscribed.

I couldn't remember any of these books ever actually being read. Seeing his work through all its stages, typing his manuscripts on the computer from indecipherable drafts time and again, proof-reading his galleys and acting as his stenographer, accountant and tax lawyer for more than ten years, it never occurred to me to just take one of his books down off the shelf and read it through as if I was a stranger picking it off a library cart or drugstore rack.

If I had, would I have recognized some secret buried in that mausoleum of words any reader with the cover price might discover at a glance? I never saw Matthew open one of the books. Or use the study. It remained sacrosanct, a shrine to himself, inviolable and useless as a tomb, while he ignored the 486 computer and continued to type his first drafts on the old black IBM Selectric he called 'The Deathstar' by the light of a goose-neck lamp in the makeshift spider-haunted work space in the basement he'd inhabited pending the completion of the study.

Laine was bargaining with a turbanned and bearded Sikh, surrounded by crates of vegetables spilled from the back of an old truck, giving it the look of a thrashed three-ton cornucopia on wheels. From the bulging bags around her ankles, she was apparently set to relieve the vitamin deficiency of the whole Lower Mainland.

"Let me guess. You're going to try to make the Guinness Book of Records for World's Largest Salad?"

"Just look at these veggies! They've still got dirt on them! They've still got this morning's dew on them, for God's sake! It's almost enough to make me turn vegan."

You'll have to, I thought as I shouldered my share of the cucumbers, lettuce, onions, cauliflowers, broccoli and cabbage, or most of it will end up down the high-performance garburator built into the dual sinks of your condo kitchen. One unfortunate guest, never invited back, dropped a silver Georgian teaspoon into that metallic maw and it had cost more to fix than a transmission overhaul on the Mini.

Not to forget the irreplaceable teaspoon, one of a set, which emerged looking like a piece of miniature modern sculpture after a plumber charging extortionate after-hours rates spent most of the evening dismantling the sinks during what was by then a very subdued dinner party. The teaspoon was saved, though. Guy, then only a dinner guest, not yet Laine's young man, came to the rescue with his skills as a gold and silver smith. Taking the mangled spoon to the shop where he was only an apprentice, he presented it, completely restored, to Laine a week later in a small box lined with a strip of black velvet. Within a week, he was her new young man.

Laine led me on a tour of the remaining outdoor dealers, both of us festooned with vegetables like a couple of fertility goddesses in a kindergarten harvest pageant.

"Marvellous bargains on garden tools."

Laine pointed to the array of rakes, hoes, wheelbarrows, mattocks, shovels, spades, pitchforks, shears, trowels, lawn-mowers gas and electric, even roto-tillers, badly battered or barely used, offered at prices I could appreciate were well below the going rate in any suburban big-box hardware chain store. It would've been catty to point out that she lived in a townhouse, caring for her few plants with nothing more than a pair of nail-scissors and a decorative brass mister, while the maintenance of the juniper shrub and bark mulch grounds of the complex was left to ever-changing crews of young men, their muscles burnished by the sun, on whom Laine would occasionally descend bearing cold beer and wearing the briefest of sun-suits when her ego was in need of a quick lift.

Looking at the tools, I suddenly missed my small back garden in Toronto. I'd laid it out and tended it so carefully. Matthew claimed growing up in the B.C. coastal rainforest put him off plants and the colour green for life. Toronto Grey was his favourite colour. I doubted he was keeping the tiny lawn watered and trimmed and the perennials would have died of neglect by now.

"There usually isn't much inside here."

Laden, we staggered into a gymnasium-sized hall housing the indoor exhibitors. Rows of trestle tables, arranged in long rectangles with the sellers inside, filled the hall from end to end. Sellers sat or stood behind their wares, drinking coffee from styrofoam cups, chatting and smoking, a separate frater-nity, almost ignoring the prospective buyers who filed past.

From what I could see as we bumped through the aisles, trying not to knock anything over with our giant unconstructed salad, Laine was right about the merchandise. This trove of bargains and treasures seemed to consist mostly of dated novelty items and remaindered kitchen gadgets as-seen-on-TV, Veg-o-Matics, Ginsu knife sets, Pet Rocks and Chia Pets, imitation Buck knives in studded imitation leather holsters, dusty dolls that walked or talked or wet their pants, lapel pins for heavy metal rock bands, huge black flags emblazoned with skeletal bikers under the legend "Ride To Live, Live To Ride" and the insignia of the Harley-Davidson motorcycle company.

Among the dull toys and improbable utensils were Lazy Susan pinwheel cut-glass pickle trays, ceramic planters in garish colours and every outlandish shape including the black panthers I remembered from the living room window-sills of neighbours' houses as a child. There were personalized coffee mugs emblazoned with unlikely names, racks of bottle-opener keychains advertising beer or auto parts, and it went on and on, a bizarre bazaar of unnecessary tools and knicknacks so manifestly ephemeral no one would ever feel more than this momentary twinge of nostalgia for them. At last, we stepped out the exit on the far side of the building into a blinding shaft of sunlight that drove us both to rummage in our purses for sunglasses. Laine snapped on her Vuarnets and lit a cigarette with an impatient gesture.

"Not much worth the trip, except the veggies, of course. We'll have to try the big indoor swap meet in Surrey."

I quickly hid my eyes behind classic Ray-Bans.

"You mean there's more?"

Chapter 4

E yes half-closed behind shades, I could ignore the King George Highway, that interminable strip of shitty motels, venal car dealerships, gas stations and fast food franchise units that passes for downtown Surrey, until a few blocks before our destination when Laine nearly ran down a hitch-hiker. He was walking down the inside lane, outside the line of parked cars. As the Porsche approached, he whirled on the thick heels of badly scuffed cowboy boots and sidestepped directly into her path, cocking a muscular forearm, thumb raised to beg a lift. He wore dirty jeans and a black t-shirt under an open, faded green and black plaid mackinaw, a garment known everywhere else in the city as a Surrey Sportsjacket.

But it wasn't his fashion sense that made me gasp and grasp the dashboard, or even the impending impact. Laine denied herself the pleasure of running him over with a quick twist of the wheel and a strident Germanic blast of the horn. She never touched the brake. As we swept past, between the ratty blonde goatee and the frayed fringe of hair across his forehead, I met a pair of eyes that glowed with a madness measurable in megawatts. His whole stance, from the sickle of a sneer that was his mouth to the bullishly hunched shoulders, was so implacably hostile that for a moment he seemed about to attack the oncoming car. I shuddered.

"My God... Did you see that?"

Laine glanced at the dwindling reflection in the rear-view mirror. "Fucking creep must be out on a day-pass."

I was still in shock. In that instant when our eyes locked, his glare had gone through me like a blade.

"But... Did you see his eyes?"

"I saw him. I should've clipped the prick and done the world a favour. Light me a cigarette, will you? These fucking Sunday drivers..."

The Porsche whined as she geared down in thickening traffic. I noticed her hand shook slightly as she reached for the short gearstick. Keeping my own hand steady, I lit one of Laine's long cigarettes and took a deep drag before passing it over. We turned into a parking lot behind a huge featureless concrete block building topped with a bedraggled banner advertising Western Canada's Biggest Indoor Swap Meet.

I didn't want to get out of the car. I knew the hitch-hiker must be at least a block and a half back. Maybe he'd even gotten a ride, though I couldn't imagine who'd pick him up. It would have to be someone even crazier and more dangerous than he was and I supposed there was bound to be one out there somewhere. You just didn't expect to encounter them on a suburban Sunday morning.

"Coming?"

Laine was standing impatiently by the open door, waiting to lock up the car, keys jangling from her fingers. I unfolded myself from the tight cockpit, suppressing a vision of the hitch-hiker running down the block, his ruined boots pounding the sidewalk like jack-hammers, knocking over bystanders too terrified to tangle with him, reaching into his pocket for the big Buck knife I imagined he must be carrying, dementedly determined to get his revenge on the two bitches in the fancy car who wouldn't give a guy a ride. I couldn't stop myself from glancing back toward the entrance of the parking lot, half-expecting to see him skid around the corner by the Pharmasave, sunlight flashing off the blade in his hand like a heliographed signal from another world.

Then we were safely inside. I paid the admission for us both this time, but again forgot to pull back my hand. A skinny lank-haired girl planted another indelible stamp on the back of my wrist. I showed it to Laine.

"If there's more of these places, I'm going to wind up looking like the Tattooed Lady."

She flaunted her own unmarked wrists.

"It'll take days to wash off. You have to learn to avoid them."

Standing in the entrance of Western Canada's Biggest Swap Meet, assaulted by the odours of oil and vinyl, mothballs and stale perspiration, foxed paper, cigarette smoke and the inexplicably strong scent of popcorn, I had no intention of learning any such thing. So far, nothing about the morning suggested it was an experience I might want to repeat. Setting my jaw, I followed Laine into the crowd, most of whom seemed sweatily over-dressed thanks to the unpredictable weather, as they picked over table after table, aisle after aisle, of the largest collection of undesirable goods I'd ever seen. It was a department store without departments, a mad market, a schizophrenic souk, filled with such a disorganized array of objects I couldn't focus on any one at a time.

I wandered blindly through the maze of fusty furniture, heaps of t-shirts advertising rock bands long dissolved, leather jackets in unfashionable cuts and colours, stacks of books by obscure authors which all seemed to have been Book Of The Month club selections no one ever read but had to keep and pay for because they neglected to send back the old computer-punched order card in time. From at least half a dozen points in the cavernous room, boom-boxes and blasters were being played to demonstrate their good working order or, it seemed, just to add to the general racket. I noticed they were all playing tapes by Creedence Clearwater Revival, though no two were playing the same song.

Weaving in and out of Fogerty's piercing treble chords were snatches of acoustic bluegrass or blues picked out by young men trying out bargain-priced guitars. One of the pickers, a seller with a table filled with instruments, was quite good, I thought. An enormously fat woman with a likewise massive perm, a seller herself, disagreed.

"Can't we have a rest from that? Isn't there enough noise in here? A person can't hardly hear themselves think!"

The question of exactly what she might hear if she ever did distracted me for a moment. Evidently sharing my thought, the guitarist smiled sardonically and winked, reprising a few bars, as if especially for me. I couldn't help smiling back. The fat woman included me in her Gorgon stare.

"Well, thank you very much!"

I scurried to keep up with Laine as the guitarist slipped the strap over his head and gave me a farewell wink. Laine was pointing to an oddly shaped two-level corner table, all slants and angles, in 1950's veneer.

"Now, wouldn't something like this be wild in your place?… It's so *Moderne*!"

I studied the table without answering immediately.

"I think it might be a bit…angular."

"Well, how about this, then?" Laine gestured to a 1930s pole lamp with its milky inverted glass shade still intact. "Do you know what these are worth? He wants seventy-five, but I'm sure we could get it for sixty, cash. Even if you decided you don't like it, you could get twice that for it downtown."

I never liked pole lamps. They throw an odd overhead glow that reminds me of my parents small, over-furnished living room. No matter how much we might get for it downtown, there was the problem of getting it there, since I didn't think a dealer who'd just been haggled down fifteen bucks would be in the mood to discuss free delivery rationally and I wasn't up to listening to another of Laine's attempts to get her own way through a bullying rant.

"I don't think so…"

Somehow I couldn't see anything in this jumble of junk in any other context but this. A fear came over me that if I took just one of these things home I might wake up to find my perfect apartment filled with unfumigated couches spotted by unidentifiable stains, unstrung tennis racquets, unplayable electric guitars, cracked dishes, mismatched glassware, burnt wood plaques displaying humourous kitchen homilies, wheel-less bicycles and badminton sets with tangled nets, battered skis, crokinole boards, ornaments and instruments of every size and description and no conceivable use. It occurred to me I should send that to Matthew as a story idea, along with the separation agreement.

Laine shot me an exasperated look which accused me of being wilfully difficult. Then she forged ahead, her head down over the tables of misbegotten merchandise, determined to examine each item. I followed wearily, staring at everything, not really seeing anything. Standing beside Laine while she considered a mirrored vanity table covered with a thick coat of revoltingly unattractive green paint, I found myself looking straight into the fierce glare of a wolverine less than four feet away. Startled, I took a sudden step back, bumping into Laine before I realized the wolverine was nothing but a scrap of old fur attached to a stuffed head whose features were fixed in that frozen snarl forever by the skill of a taxidermist. Laine gave me a puzzled look.

"Sorry."

Laine eyed the wolverine with an even sterner look of disapproval than she'd given me over the pole lamp.

"We're talking about an apartment, babe. Not a hunting lodge. It's worth a girl's life just to wear leather skirts these days, let alone her furs. Everyone's a member of a committee to get some kind of vermin on or off the Endangered Species List. First time you host a party, a girl who came with somebody will spend the whole evening holding forth in a very loud voice about how many years ago she quit eating red meat and how her overwhelming reverence for life has caused her to subsist on a very moral diet of aptly named mung beans. Just as you're serving the teriyaki steak tidbits, she'll launch into a graphic description of a furry creature gnawing off its leg to escape from a trap or a detailed recital of industrial slaughterhouse procedures… No, it won't do, though I wouldn't mind it in my office, if I could have it installed in a box so it would just pop up at the touch of a button."

I tried to smile, but the heat and the thick, stale air, the sour smell of the crowd and the permeating odour of popcorn, the squalling of children and husbands and wives bickering in low tones over why one of them would want to add yet another piece of junk to the mess in the garage or basement, the steady jangle of CCR tunes from cheap tinny speakers were all combining to make me feel more than slightly sick.

Laine looked at me sharply.

"Eve? You alright? You look a bit off-white."

"I really think I should sit down…"

"Are you getting your period?"

Laine managed to turn a few nearby heads with that one. I shook my head. Laine took my arm anyway.

"Look, there's a coffee counter over in that corner. Why don't you just toddle over and sit down for a minute. I just want to see if I can beat this bandit down enough to make it worthwhile having the paint stripped off this lovely old thing. It would look wonderful in my boudoir."

I did as I was told, catching a glimpse of my pallid reflection in the big mirror flanked by pedestal cabinets as I passed. Refinished, it would have looked nice in my own nearly empty bedroom, but the original purpose of our expedition seemed to have been forgotten for the moment. I found the coffee counter after a frustrating meander through the idly shuffling crowd. It was just an improvised bar serving a brew so black and deadly one sip from the styrofoam cup was an endorsement of herbal teas. Despite my earlier caffeine overload, I pined for my Mr. Coffee and a mug of Kenyan Roast. A few folding tables surrounded by mismatched chairs completed the cafe. Having found an unoccupied table and a reasonably steady chair, I contemplated an overflowing pressed-tin ashtray that killed my desire for a cigarette.

That was when I saw him.

Fumbling for my sunglasses with shaking fingers, I looked away so quickly I could hardly believe it and had to look again from behind the dubious protection of ultraviolet blocking lenses. It was him alright. The hitch-hiker we had almost killed was lurching away from the counter, a steaming white cup wrapped in thick fingers scarred by blurred blue jailhouse tattoos, glaring with undiluted belligerence at every occupied table where there was a vacant chair, silently demanding an invitation and daring anyone to tell him the seat was taken.

Staring down at the muddy surface of my coffee, I prayed he would sit somewhere else, go away, that the ground would open up and swallow him or me, that a major earthquake or nuclear strike would level the building. But I knew, the way you know when the weirdo gets on the bus and the seat beside you is empty, he would choose me with the unerring instinct of the predator for the victim, the weak one, the one who would not have the courage to escape. Someone was standing beside the table. I couldn't look up.

Laine slid into the chair opposite.

"God, Eve. You do look like yesterday's lingerie. Are you sure it's not your period? I mean, you're not pregnant or anything stupid and girlish, are you?"

I let out the breath I hadn't been aware of holding. It seemed like forever before I could breathe in again. I still couldn't bring myself to look up and my voice was a hoarse croak.

"It's…him…"

Laine looked around.

"Him? Him *who*? What *are* you talking about?"

I hissed her quiet.

"That hitch-hiker! Don't look around!"

Laine's head snapped up and around like she expected to see someone who owed her money.

"What? Where?… I don't see him."

I raised my eyes slowly. The hitch-hiker had vanished. There was an exit to the parking lot a few steps away. Unable to find a find a free table, he must've gone outside.

"He was here…"

Moving the full ashtray to the next table with a gesture of disgust, Laine lit a cigarette with a flourish which announced her intention to flick her ashes on the floor until the service improved.

"You look like you need some fresh air. There's nothing here today but tat and crap anyway. Come on, we'll stop at the Terminal Avenue Flea Market on the way home. Do you want to finish your coffee?"

I shook my head.

"No… But what if he's still outside? In the parking lot?"

I managed not to say *waiting*.

"Who? That hitch-hiking fuckwit? He's just some low-rent local white trash. Forget him. If he is out there, it'll be the sorriest fucking day of his life."

With that, she rose and marched toward the door.

Chapter 5

The hitch-hiker wasn't in the parking lot. Safe in the car again, I'd almost stopped searching the sunstruck sidewalks for his swaggering gait and savage smile as we drove away. Then he appeared, a hundred yards ahead, in our lane, threatening passing cars with his thumb as if it held the hammer of a cocked revolver. My throat closed like a probed anemone.

"Laine!"

"I see him."

Downshifting into second, Laine stomped the gas like a dragstrip driver getting the green light. With a turbo-charged growl the Porsche pounced. I lost my grip on the dash as the acceleration slammed me back in the contoured bucket seat.

"Laine?"

For a moment, I actually believed the hitcher wasn't going to move. Retracting his thumb and balling his fists, he faced down the speeding car with bunched shoulders and lowered brows, his snarling face mimicking the frozen grimace of the stuffed wolverine, as if he expected to force us off the road with nothing more than the irresistible laser power of his own rage.

I shut my eyes in denial, opening them just in time to see him fling himself to the side in a near Olympic-class Western Roll across the trunk of a parked car. Then we were past, long gone as Laine slewed the Porsche expertly in and out of traffic, checking her mirrors to make sure no cops had witnessed her attempt at vehicular homicide. I waited until I felt calm enough to light cigarettes for both of us before I said anything.

"Why did you do that?"

Mistress of the French inhale, Laine sucked thick twin streams of exhaled smoke back into her flaring nostrils.

"To teach him a lesson. Punks like that are only as tough as you let them be. You can't take any shit at all from them, or from anybody, for that matter. You've got to realize, Eve, the sweet little girl routine works fine on the runway, in cover shots and commercials, but it won't get you around the block in one piece in the real world."

I took a deep drag on my cigarette and settled back in the bucket seat. I'd been listening to variations on this theme for months, ever since Laine appointed herself den mother and confidante as well as employer. But Laine was using a different on-ramp this time.

"Most people aren't terribly special, not nearly as unique as they think. They eat, drink, shit, sleep and fuck, make money and reproduce their own failings in their children. There's really nothing they do that couldn't be done just as well by somebody else. As long as they don't see it, as long as they think they're special just for being alive, everything's fine. But some of them are just smart enough to figure out they're nothing special and knowing it makes them feel like less than nothing. It puts a chip on their shoulders. Like your friend back there. He can walk out into traffic because he knows he's got nothing to lose anybody wants. If he makes an expensive powerful car he could never hope to own swerve out of his way, it makes him feel like a big man for a minute, instead of the insignificant little shit-stain on a paper towel he knows he really is… I wish I *had* hit him."

"Laine, you don't mean that…"

"Of course I do. I'd've been doing everyone a favour, including him."

I thought about that as I smoked too much during the drive back into the city. Was there anything I could do that couldn't be done just as well by someone else? Was there anything I did that really made the slightest difference to the world whether it got done or not? I'd had that argument with my analyst.

Originally, Dr. Stern was the marriage counsellor I talked Matthew into seeing when the accumulated poisons of a decade and a half together erupted into a festering wound that wouldn't heal, when the all-night discussions left us both exhausted, too tired for tears, sitting on the stairs drinking scotch until we could safely get into bed without caring if we brushed against each other in the dark.

Dr. Stern was a large dark-haired woman who dressed in tailored skirts and peasant blouses and embroidered vests in bright primary colours, acquired on the trips she frequently made to Third World countries. The walls of her office, painted in a faux sandstone wash, displayed Navajo rugs and small

Afghan prayer carpets. Inuit carvings and fragments of pre-Columbian pottery posed beside Dogon sculpture on the bookshelves and the French-polished expanse of her antique desk, whose curved legs culminated in heavy tapered claws, each clutching a large ball. A pair of muscular Boxer dogs disposed themselves on the floor, alert but apparently docile, between their mistress and her patients.

During our second session, when the Doctor questioned Matthew about his lack of participation, he ignored her query and asked about the dogs.

"Do these dogs have to be here?"

Doctor Stern smiled patiently.

"This is my office. It is my space. These are my dogs. They are quite harmless, I assure you…But we were talking about the importance of real communication, weren't we Matthew?"

Dr. Stern always called her patients by their first names. We, however, were to call her "Doctor," she informed us at the outset, to preserve her neutral objectivity and remind us that we had a problem and she was a professional who might help us solve it, not a family friend. Matthew flicked a Camel cigarette out of the small pack into the corner of his mouth and I cringed. The Doctor smiled again.

"I have requested you refrain from smoking during these sessions. These dogs are subject to asthmatic attacks and so am I. Nicotine may help you to relax temporarily, but you are not here to relax, are you, Matthew? You are here to talk honestly about your relationship. Yes?"

I heard the soft metallic ping of his cherished old Zippo and enviously caught a whiff of thick, rich Turkish and American tobacco smoke. The dogs' furrowed foreheads frowned in unison as Matthew's exhaled sigh filled the room with a rolling cloud of fragrant poisons.

"I don't want to talk about relationships. I just want to have one."

Doctor Stern shook her head, wagging a forefinger toward a heavy stone bowl on the corner of the desk. It looked like Mayan women had spent a few thousand years grinding corn in it.

"I must insist that you do not smoke in this office."

Matthew got up slowly and sauntered to the door, exhaling another toxic thunderhead of second-hand smoke. For a moment, I was afraid the Doctor would utter some secret word of command and galvanize the tense dogs into snarling, murderously programmed rage, that Matthew would be torn to pieces in the vestibule of the chic office.

"Coming?"

Matthew waited at the door. It took all my strength to shake my head without turning around. If I'd gone with him then, I'd never again have been able to suggest anything about our relationship was less than ideal for fear of having all this, the Doctor, the intimidating dogs, the childish rules, thrown back at me. Not in words so much as in one of Matthew's devastatingly articulate looks as he lit up a Camel. The door clicked firmly shut behind him.

"I'm sorry."

Doctor Stern shook her head briskly, waving away the roiling smoke.

"The first thing you must do is to stop apologizing for things you have not done. Matthew's childish self-destructive behaviour has embarrassed you, but that is not your fault. Is it? Now perhaps we can begin…"

But I was no longer paying attention to the Doctor's projected plans for future sessions. I was thinking about David in Vancouver. A session with him would begin with a tart, dry Margarita, segue to a simple but superb menu of pesto-brushed chicken on a bed of noodles moistened with Alfredo sauce, escorted by grilled zucchini, cherry tomatoes and baby carrots. The cork would be drawn from a perfectly oaked Californian or Chilean chardonnay to lubricate the meal, then... But that was before Carolyn's hyperactive ovaries turned him into someone I no longer thought about except as the putative sire of another spoiled yuppie-pup nursed on hypo-allergenic soy milk, spoon-fed miso soup and Thai rice congee instead of pablum, destined to grow up to ruthlessly dominate its parents and commit them to a seniors gulag as soon as the ink dried on the power of attorney.

The Terminal Avenue Flea Market was actually a relief after the racetrack auditoriums and abandoned supermarkets of the suburbs. The long red barn of a building was a cathedral of cast-offs, but I was reassured by the flimsy siding, whose cracks admitted slices of sunlight, comforted by the knowledge that I was at least back in the centre of the city. If I wanted, I could step outside, hop a bus and be back in my apartment in less than half an hour. A cab would take ten minutes.

By the time I had my hand stamped for the third time, by a Sikh with a fierce but kindly smile, I'd got the knack of following Laine out of the corner of one eye while I gazed vacantly over table after table of remaindered Made in Hong Kong sweatshop souvenirs, tinny wind-chimes and novelties that were anything but novel, most of them still sealed in original plastic, grimy with age and the careless storage that is the lot of unwanted things, presided over by chain-smoking

Chinese as impassive as Buddhas.

Partitioned down the centre, the extended building seemed to go on forever, turning back on itself like an Escher print, a labyrinth of aisles heaped with untidy piles of unidentifiable things, an endless chamber of anterooms filled with unauthenticated antiques, scabrous furniture, worn out clothes, bicycles with bent frames, skis with broken bindings, stained sleeping bags, purposeless tools. This was the infinite closet of Hell. The smells of old grease, older dust, naptha and aged sweat hung in the nicotine-blue air. Beside me, two men argued over what looked like a medieval weapon.

"Puffeckly good ize-axe. Onny fordy bucks. Cost you a hundert anywheres elze."

"It hasn't got a ferrule."

"Whaz?"

"The ferrule. The knob you attach to the wrist-loop."

"Well… Is why is onny fordy bucks."

Laine materialized at my elbow.

"Look at this! Don't you just love it?"

She fanned a book under my nose, filling my sinuses with the dry stale scent of aged cheap paper. I caught a glimpse of the title. *Swingin' Shindig! Dance Your Way Into The In Crowd!*

Inside were black and white photographs of young men and women from the early Sixties, the men in hip-hugging high-waisted bell-bottom pants, frilled shirts and Cuban-heeled boots, the women in A-line mini-dresses, patterned stockings and sling-back shoes, sporting white lipstick and lacquered bouffant hairdos. With fixed smiles, they were frozen like living hieroglyphs in a series of static poses so bizarre they suggested some ecstatic religious rite as they demonstrated the authorized performance of The Monkey,

The Swim, The Loco-Motion and The Jerk.

Laine didn't even look at the man who emerged from a crowd of chatting vendors to stand behind the trestle table, but snapped over her shoulder.

"How much do you want for this?"

He looked at her thoughtfully from under his short, thinning blonde hair.

"Usually I'd ask two bucks, but I'm not sure I want to part with it."

Laine turned on him as though he'd just suggested she hike up her skirt and pass the Vaseline. Her eyes widened. Her nostrils flared. One fist clenched itself against her hip. For an infinitely extended moment, she seemed to be in shock. Yet this wasn't just the familiar acid-wash she turned on waiters and sales staff who failed to accord her the respect she claimed as her due. It was as if she'd been overcome, possessed by an instant loathing of this innocuous-looking guy.

"I …beg…your…pardon?"

The man took the book from her suddenly limp hand and leafed through it.

"I said, I might not want to sell it to you."

I took a long curious look at this nondescript guy who seemed so uncannily and deliberately oblivious to Laine's furious posturing, absorbed in the book as though it was a priceless ancient manuscript. His hair was cropped as if to emphasize rather than hide his premature pattern-baldness. Neither young nor old, his face had a recently weatherbeaten look, not coarsened by a lifetime outdoors. His clothes looked like he'd shopped for them right here at the flea market. His clean-shaven face maintained an expression of absolute seriousness as he scrutinized the cheap volume.

Finally he put the book down on the table in front of him, where a number of equally disparate articles were arranged—a record of The Chipmunks Cha-Cha Party, an assortment of videos of old science-fiction and horror movies, a small black and white TV tuned to an evangelical broadcast with the sound turned down, a rounded stainless steel two-slice toaster whose Bakelite handle had suffered a slight crack and a portable tape player that was softly emitting what sounded like the greatest hits of Jimi Hendrix performed by an orchestra of kazoo-players stoned on Quaaludes. He shook his head.

"No. I don't want to sell this to you."

His emphasis on the personal pronouns was unmistakable. Laine immediately adopted the no-nonsense tone she used with panhandlers, cretins, ass-grabbers, actors sulking over zits and models too shy to do lingerie.

"Look. This is a flea market. I assume you paid someone five or ten bucks or whatever for this table, on which you have placed various articles for sale. Things you have acquired in some presumably legal manner and now wish to re-sell at a profit. I am a customer. I have expressed a wish to purchase this book, which you have offered for sale." Picking up the book with one hand, she flipped her Buxton Executive wallet out of her purse. "Now, I believe you said two dollars…"

The man ignored the shiny two-dollar coin she waved back and forth under his nose like a hypnotist trying to subdue a trance-resistant subject.

"It's not the money. You see, a lot of people buy these kinds of things on impulse, as a joke. But by the time they get home, the joke isn't funny anymore, or it's only funny for a day or two. Then the thing gets thrown in a drawer or a box or stuck away somewhere. The person who has it forgets they even have it and the people who might really want it and enjoy it never even get to see it until the person gives it away to the Sally Ann or the Handicapped Thrift Shop or someplace where a dealer might spot it. Or else, they throw it away in the garbage, in which case it's gone forever…"

He spoke with the sadness of a classical scholar describing remnants of the poems of Sappho after the burning of the great Library of Alexandria, torn up for Egyptian grocery lists and memo pads, then tossed on a Cairo landfill to rot.

"How much did you pay for this table?"

He shrugged.

"Five bucks."

With a conjurer's deftness, a crisp five dollar bill appeared in Laine's hand. Her wallet always seemed to contain bills fresh from the mint. I wondered if she actually changed her scruffy bills for new ones at the bank. I had actually seen her over-tip to avoid taking crumpled or dirty bills as change.

"Here. I've bought your table for the day. Now, may I have the book?"

He hesitated, regarding Laine with a look I found unfathomable. Then he dropped his eyes and shrugged. Laine let the bill and the coin fall to the table and snugged the book under her arm as she whirled on one heel and stalked away.

Secretly I'd been hoping he would thwart Laine's whim at any cost. I hoped to see him hold out against the considerable weight of cash and credit she could muster, that he'd tell her he did not take Gold MasterCard, Platinum Visa, American or even Arabian Express, that he'd drive her into a bidding frenzy, offering cheques, comped concert tickets, a date with a famous model, the promise of a blowjob or other submissive sexual favour, the mortgage on her Kits townhouse, anything, to obtain the coveted book. As I turned away, he gave me an odd rueful smile. When I caught up with Laine, she was triumphantly smug but over-acting the part.

"I told you this would be fun." It was always fun when Laine got her own way, but something in her voice wasn't making it. "What shall we do now?"

"We could get out of here."

"Well, yes. I suppose we might as well. You've looked a bit off all day and it hasn't been terribly successful, has it? We didn't get a thing for your apartment."

She agreed with what seemed like unseemly speed. In the narrow curbside parking lot, squinting against the acetylene brilliance of the sun, I was digging for my Ray-Bans when Laine, Vuarnets already in place, abruptly turned on me with regenerate manic glee.

"I know! We'll have a proper house-warming party! Everyone will bring things! Everyone we know has reliable taste, after all, and what you absolutely can't live with, you can exchange. I'll fix it up for next weekend. A sort of late afternoon, early evening, cocktail thingie, so those who have dinner dates or theatre tickets can still make it. You can handle the *hors*, right? Your crab dip is always a hit. And"—she brandished the precious book like the Queen Witch flaunting a Lucifer-autographed copy of the *Malleus Maleficarium*—"I'll bring some oldies tapes! We'll do the Twist! We can Mashed Potato! We can do The Jerk! It'll be a blast from the past!"

Too tired to resist, I slumped in my seat as we navigated the sad seething blocks of Main Street. I barely saw the Three Lizard cooking wine connoisseurs and the girl junkies telling men they hadn't eaten in three days, as if the thought of what such a girl might do with a piece of meat in her mouth would make them slow their money-stride, the panhandlers mechanically mumbling litanies for spare change like mendicant monks, the three-string out of tune guitar players groaning "House of the Rising Sun" or "Been Through the Desert on a Horse With No Name" beside pub doorways, the mental patients dumped on the sidewalks by government cutbacks pushing bent shopping carts filled with garbage salvaged from dumpsters, babbling, whooping, ranting, threatening, crying at nothing and everything.

As we passed the Cobalt Hotel, my head snapped around as one eye caught a flash of blonde hair, the muddy green plaid pattern of a mackinaw disappearing into the dark entrance of a pub that slammed as quickly and finally as the gates of Hades.

No, I told myself. That would be just too much for one day.

Chapter 6

I still felt shrivelled when I parked the Mini in the old Woodwards Parkade and willed all the energy remaining in my body into my calves so I could briskly trot up the single flight of slate-tiled stairs with the Monday morning enthusiasm expected of staff at The Agency. As the heavy glass door with its calligraphic brushwork lettering automatically swung shut, my low heels announced me. High or narrow heels were forbidden for fear of distressing the original distressed wood warehouse floors. Tardiness was audible in Laine's huge office at the rear with its panoramic view of Burrard Inlet and the North Shore mountains.

"Eve?"

Christ, it was only ten minutes. Was she going to twist her French silk knickers over less time than it took to smoke a plain-end cigarette?

"Coming."

I turned on one heel away from the sanctuary of my own small office with its loop-hole view of Water Street and crossed from polished wood onto the long abstract Kilim runner which led to Laine's command centre. Her door was always open, she liked to tell clients.

True, though she neglected to mention the open door enabled her to monitor office traffic, cut down on employee gossip and impressed those waiting on the beige Italian leather couches perusing a selection of the latest sub-cult mags and fanzines by allowing them to eavesdrop on her phone conversations apparently with major players on the international fashion and entertainment scenes. The unheard computer-generated voice of Environment Canada's regional weather update might be on the other end of the line for all they knew, but Laine had been relentlessly ripping the scales from my eyes with hot tweezers since I moved from the runway to the backstage.

"We don't have to believe in our clients, but they have to believe in us. They wouldn't be paying us if they didn't believe we can make other people believe they're beautiful and talented. Even the ones who truly are, are really feebs or they wouldn't be paying our fees. They think they need our connections, our push, and our job is to keep them thinking it…

"So if Sly Stallone is shooting in town and his manager calls me to get some of our clients to upgrade the crowd at some club the big salami will be gracing with his presence after a day on the set, don't be surprised if you hear *that* conversation on the speaker-phone coming out of my office a dozen times that day on tape. It's just business. And when the clients at reception hear it, every one of them will be sitting on the edge of the chair when they get in here, squirming like girls at a high school sock-hop waiting to be asked to dance. Whatever neurotic insecure shit they've come in to whine about will be completely forgotten as they hum and haw, waiting for me to say, 'Oh, Sly's hosting a little casual apres-shoot thing tonight. Why don't you come along?'... If they've been a hemorroid lately, I let them sweat and make chit-chat until they start dropping the desperate hints, 'I hear Sly's in town,' before I say, 'Oh yeah. He wants to meet some local talent. Always on the lookout for new faces, underexposed co-stars who won't upstage him by having more screen presence than a door-jamb. Why don't you drop in? Could be good for you to mingle with his LA people.' The closest they're going to get to Stallone is blowing his local hair-stunt-double in the john, but they crawl out of here hyperventilating and creaming their custom-ripped jeans with joy and gratitude, congratulating themselves on the extreme good fortune that allowed them to become clients of The Agency... And that's what it's all about."

Laine was dangerously mellow. Her "Good morning how are you?" was warm, but a little wan, as if she'd been playing the Boomtown Rats "I Don't Like Mondays" over her fruit and nut granola too, but was genuinely more concerned about how my week was starting. Nothing like the chilly "Good afternoon" which usually prefaced her conversations with anyone more than five minutes late. I was *en garde* instantly.

"Eve? I need to ask you an absolutely huge favour."

This was good. If Laine said it was absolutely huge, it was really a small thing, which she would later rave over with extravagant gratitude because everyone would know you hadn't really done anything much by the time she re-told it, but you'd still be seen to be the lucky recipient of her displays of affection and some extravagant gift which demonstrated her sensitivity to the smallest details. Truly Big Things were discussed In Strict Confidence and Behind Closed Doors and Who Owed Who What never alluded to except in the fine print of contracts.

"Anything, Laine.You know that."

She sighed dramatically.

"I've got a full rack, back to back meetings all week, so naturally this is the week kids in Lisa's class at school have to spend a couple of days with their parents learning about what they do at their jobs…" She grabbed a fistful of her hair without overly dismaying her coiffure. "So the teachers are all off at some retreat rubbing each other down with scented oils and getting in touch with the Mentoring Spirit Within while the parents get to baby-sit. Our tax dollars at work. It's my fault. She told me and I forgot and scheduled all these things for this week. If I take her with me… Well, I can't take her with me and you know why. Even if she could hear, she wouldn't understand ninety-nine percent of what's being said. So I should bring along someone who can translate all this contract shit into sign language so she can know how bored shitless she is? It just won't work and I think her class would probably find the modelling classes and photo shoots a lot more interesting than contract negotiations… And since you're just the *very* best person I have doing that… Would you mind awfully? Being Mom for a couple of days? Just letting Lisa be part of your day?…I know it's a lot to ask…"

I sighed inside, relief and exasperation about fifty-fifty.

"No problem, Laine. I'd be happy to have Lisa with me. She already knows the basics anyway…" Then, instead of leaving well enough alone, I dropped the teaspoon down the sink, metaphorically. "I don't suppose she could spend the days with her father… I mean, since its supposed to be a parental thing…"

Laine's face froze in a frightening mask. She couldn't have gone from glad to mad faster if I'd reached across the dustless glass-topped desk and tweaked her tits nestled in their contoured La Senza cups. She shot me a sharp demanding look.

"What do you mean by that?"

"Nothing…just… Look, forget it. I said…"

"Obviously I can't let her spend time with her father, under the circumstances."

She laid a lot of escaping stress on the last phrase, blatantly searching my face for any sign I knew what she was talking about. I played dumb, which was easy enough.

"Laine, last time you told me anything about him, and that was a few years ago, you said he was working at some cheap hotel. I wasn't thinking. Obviously that's not someplace you want Lisa to be spending time…"

She slammed her shoulders back into the ergonomic embrace of her chair.

"He couldn't even hold a job getting other drunks drunk. The next time I see his name I want it to be in the obituary column of some tabloid I wouldn't ask my Burmese to use as litter. As for Lisa, she can lip-read and if anyone around here so much as says the word 'father,' a sidewalk stroll in Mount Pleasant will look like a viable career option."

"Laine, I'm sorry I even mentioned it. I didn't mean anything by it, it just popped out. I'll be happy to have Lisa as my assistant for a few days. I'll see to it she has a great time and gets an A on the project. After all you've done for me, it'll be a pleasure, believe me."

Gratitude expressed, balance of power restored, Laine relaxed with effort and forced a smile.

"Sorry, Evie. I'm over-reacting. I've just got a brutal week ahead and Lisa's father is the last person I have a split second to waste thinking about. I knew you wouldn't let me down. I picked Lisa up on the way in. She's down the hall having cappucino with Gail. I'll leave the two of you to get on with it, shall I?"

Dismissed, I stood up and got out of there before I could put my other foot in my mouth. Why Lisa's father should suddenly become a recurrent irritating panty rash when Laine herself often referred to him casually as "Lisa's sperm donor" or "the prick I was married to until I discovered it had a personality" when she was pumped at a party, or "my ex, as in ex-crement," which she found funny after the fifth glass of wine on the balcony late at night, I had no idea.

Dutifully I collected Lisa from the coffee room. Her mood seemed to mirror my own. We'd been dumped on each other and we both knew it. In spite of the awkwardness we felt, I was surprised again by the beauty that peeked out from behind the polite but sullen mask. She was what? Fourteen? Leggy as a newborn colt, she'd already done some Junior Miss catalogue work, decorous bathing suits and panties and training bras for the pre-bikini wax set.

You could see why photographers like Chris Newman were after Laine to let her work more. She wasn't beautiful yet, but she would be and photographers can't help but be intrigued by a subject who extends the microsecond frame of the photograph. Chris once tried to explain his theory of photographing subjects who extend the frame to me over too many glasses of wine.

"Still photographs capture a split second in time. Most of them capture only that, one second isolated by the shutter. But certain faces, girls on the verge of womanhood, women on the verge of middle age, old men who've lived hard, farmed the land or been to sea, can express much more than the instant actually caught on film… Their faces and bodies convey a sense of everything that has happened or will happen to them. Those pictures are worth more than a thousand words. They're like whole volumes of history condensed and burned into a single image…"

Lisa had a book under her arm. She always had a book under her arm. One of the reasons Laine gave to explain pushing her daughter into modelling was that she was afraid Lisa's deafness was turning her into some kind of introverted bookworm.

"She's always got her nose in some damn book or other and they're not Nancy Drew mysteries either. The other day I caught her reading two books at once, for fuck sake. One was about ancient Greek mythology and the other was a bunch of very weird short stories by some blind South American writer who probably used to write episodes of *The Twilight Zone*. I read the jacket blurbs and a few pages because you're supposed to know what your children are reading, but it's fucking nonsense. I don't want her escaping into fairy tales from the past or twee science fiction. I'd be happier if she was reading shit like *Valley of the Doll*s or funny crap like *Bridget Jones Diary*. At least they don't pretend to represent some alternative higher reality of the soul fucked up losers can be suckered into believing in."

Laine was a patron of the arts. The halls and walls of The

Agency were decked with works she bought on the advice of her contacts at the Emily Carr Institute, whose annual graduate show she did a cyclone sweep through with notebook and chequebook, buying up the works of future geniuses at bargain prices. Yet she could raise welts on a rock talking about artists and assume she was playing to a hometown crowd with me because, after all, hadn't I dumped a husband largely because he believed more in the reality of his art, his words and his stories, than he did in the real story of his life with me?

Lisa's precocious love of books didn't seem peculiar to me. In books, it doesn't matter if you're deaf. All you have to grasp is the difference made by quotation marks, between what people think and what they actually say and do. If you get that, you can be deaf as a stone without losing a single nuance of modern or postmodern irony. Literature is a world of eloquent silence.

While Matthew and I were de-constructing our marriage, one of our rare moments of hysterical giggling agreement occurred on the night we compared notes and discovered that both his male friends and my female friends had given us identical advice: have a child together.

"Knock her up… Keep her barefoot and pregnant in the kitchen."

"Forget your pill. Get pregnant. He'll see you in a totally new way and when he's in the delivery room after watching you suffer for twelve hours to squirt the bloody, mucky fruit of his loins into his arms, he'll turn into Ward Cleaver and be your worshipful slave for life."

The reason I hadn't done it was sitting right across from me.

My girl friends and Matthew's guy friends were right and

knowing it gave me a brief sense of power. Matthew wrote to create a world he could control. By having a child, I could take away that control, trap him in a world in which he would be forever vulnerable. He might not be my worshipful slave, but he would be the child's. And like my Italian next door neighbour Lucia in Toronto, who passed over the fence presents of bottles filled with strong wine from garage grapes, or puree she rendered from plum tomatoes in her verdant back garden, Lucia, whose womb was busier than a city bus terminal, her cervix a revolving door, I could rule a kingdom without moving more than a foot from the cradle tucked beside the warm kitchen stove, be a queen with a sauce-reddened sceptre, splay-footed in a splattered slip with a regalia of garlic cloves and pacifiers. Mother, she who must be honoured if not always obeyed.

But across from me sat the beautiful nightmare, the genetic tossed coin that defies the odds and lands on edge, neither heads nor tails, the sperm and ova that tumble like loaded dice off the table and land askew—the flawed child. Every one of the parents who told us to have a child together admitted their worst fear was not that their children might miscarry or be stillborn, but that one might damaged, deformed, defective in some way, afflicted with Downs Syndrome, cystic fibrosis, spina bifida, and yet live.

I knew most people thought I was just vain, afraid pregnancy would distort the body and face I'd shaped into a career, but it wasn't that at all. I was afraid alright, afraid my perfect body might betray itself by producing a child that was less than perfect.

Grabbing a Pilot FineLiner from the ceramic *en pointe* ballet shoe that held my pens and markers, I scribbled a message to Lisa on a tearaway memo.

You've already done most of this stuff so it will be easy! You're going to get an A and we're going to have fun!

The corners of her mouth turned down. Taking her own ballpoint gel-pen from her purse she neatly printed her reply under my scribble and pushed the note back.

I think this whole business is creepy. I don't want to do any more modelling. I'm going to be a writer.

My Swedish-designed minimalist steno desk chair poked me sharply in the back as I sagged into it.

Chapter 7

L isa and I survived the week because we both knew Laine well enough to give her exactly what she wanted. Lisa was attentive and co-operative during the classes. Despite her declaration, she endured being photographed as a demo model by an insouciantly amused Chris Newman. It was Laine's idea that the pics would be included with Lisa's essay and she was right. Gail the receptionist laser-printed the graphic-enhanced text written by Lisa, a convincingly girlish account of her model for a day experience, including quotes from me purporting to be Laine. Once it was assembled, with Chris' eight-by-ten glossies in one of The Agency's signature burgundy binders, it was impossible to imagine Lisa getting less than an A+ on the assignment.

Lisa pursed her lips slightly, then tucked the immaculate presentation under her arm and waited until Laine and Gail, properly thanked, left my office. Then she offered me her hand. There was something in it, a few sheets of paper, neatly folded into a scroll tied with a black ribbon. I took it, along with the enveloped note on handmade paper. Another Laine touch, making sure her daughter knew how to write a bread and butter note, right down to the artisan stationary.

Thank you, Eve, for all your help with my school project. PS. The story is just for you.

I tucked the roll of paper into my purse.

"Thank you, Lisa. I'll read it later."

It was Friday and all I had to do for the party tomorrow was prepare a decadently rich and expensive crab mousse, artichoke hearts wrapped in bacon with a sour cream and fresh dill relish, hot spicy Buffalo chicken wings with softened blue cheese for dipping, homemade blender salsa and guacamole, and enough jalapeno Monterey Jack cheese to melt over a mountain of corn chips. In spite of the lightness of the fare, the groceries, a couple of bottles of Cipes Brut pyramid-aged bubbly and backup litres of cheap Italian Trebbiano and Sangiovese di Romagna made a substantial dent in my house-keeping budget.

Shopping and prep took up most of Friday night and Saturday afternoon. Saturday morning was spent at Granville Island Public Market, blowing more money on fresh ingredients for a fruit plate and drinking espresso, which made me feel exhausted by the time I got home. Usually I loved the preparations, the fussing and making everything just so. Matthew even managed to find fault with that.

"Why do we *have* to use matching china and matching fucking napkins when there's only two of us eating Szechuan take-out, for Christ sake?" So much for my attempt to make every meal a celebration of living, as the magazines say. I never enjoyed the actual parties I hostessed after the first hour or so. Watching guests munch, careless of crumbs, drop half-chewed chicken bones into ashtrays and plant pots, leave scummy bent toothpick skewers on mantlepieces and side-boards, butt cigarettes in decoratively sliced tomatoes or watermelon, was anti-climactic to the point of nausea.

I didn't expect help from Laine. In spite of a gourmet kitchen boasting every kitchen utensil known to international cuisine, she claimed not to be able to boil water. Under torture, she might admit she could cook brunch, but had no desire to extend her repertoire. I had assumed I'd have help from Michael. Among his many accomplishments, he was completely at ease in a kitchen. His cheese souffles invited angels to recline, he could discuss recipes as comfortably as modern art or Norton motorcyles. But Michael begged off, pleading a meeting on Friday evening and a lot of errands scheduled for Saturday. He would be at the party, he assured me, because one of his errands was to take delivery of the present he'd ordered especially for me the moment Laine called.

True to his word, he arrived a little early, wanting to be the first he said, and presented me with a complete professional *flambé* set in copper and brass which must have cost hundreds per piece. He'd ordered it through his friend Jacques, owner of a cosy Parisien style West End bistro where he had taken me for late night *steak frites*. Putting my arms around him and attempting a longish, properly grateful kiss, I murmured something about inaugurating it at breakfast. He disengaged himself with deliberate mock-horror and a not so deliberate mock smile.

"Steak Diane for breakfast?"

I'd been about to say that it depended entirely on what

time you finally got around to breakfast when Laine arrived, champagne, Sixties tapes and dance book in hand, with the howling pack hard on her celebratory high heels. I calculated I'd more than broken even financially as the gifts piled up. Crystal wine glasses and highballs in sets of four. Matching balloon snifters for brandy and liqueur shooters. Laine had chosen the pattern and obviously advised the guests. Sensible and understated, none of your Scottish pinwheels or Viennese tints trimmed in gold. Stacks of immaculate pastel towels in shades that matched my shower curtain, Henckel knives you could perform major surgery with, an elegant sake set, and a pole lamp in mint condition, which I hated on sight. From Chris, Amanda's soon-to-be-ex, an authentic Sixties lava-lamp which he proclaimed was more interesting than television.

The girls from The Agency, Laine, the other agents and secretaries, had chipped in for the obligatory joke gift, a deluxe variable-speed Personal Massage Unit whose real purpose was too obvious. One of the girls squealed in delight.

"It's Bob!"

"Bob?"

"Bob! The Battery Operated Boyfriend! Saviour of the single girl!"

Turned on, the unit emitted a low buzz that was vaguely menacing, yet somehow funny as a cartoon because it could be silenced with a flick of a finger. I christened it 'Buzz' instead of Bob, in memory of the fifteen-year-old guy I had my first serious crush on. He worked part-time at a Chevron station and looked too cool to live in big grease-stained blue overalls that hung on him like a caftan. Naturally Buzz was the hit of the party, with Laine and the girls making stage-whispered queries about time-sharing privileges whenever I was "fully satisfied" Buzz was in good working order. I threw a less than subtle glance in Michael's direction.

"Anytime, ladies. I don't think I'll be needing him very often…"

More laughter greeted this, but there was a catty note to it, something arch and too knowing in the glances that flicked around the room like throwing knives. From Amanda, who arrived late and alone, I received a designer sheet and pillow-case set which, I couldn't help noticing, was for a single bed. I wondered briefly how Amanda, who'd never been in my apartment, knew I slept in a single. Had she asked Laine? Or Michael? He left the room to fetch Amanda a drink as I opened that particular present and avoided my eyes when he returned with a glass of the unmistakably golden boutique California chardonnay I assumed he'd brought for us to share.

I didn't have time to think about it or talk to Michael. Laine recruited him to help her demonstrate the dances illustrated in the book she'd paid such an outrageous price to possess. A deejay friend who worked at one of the dominant 'classic rock' stations downtown had made her tapes of all the original dance hits, dances no one would admit remembering for fear of dating themselves, but in no time everyone was passing the book around and getting into The Swim, The Pony, The Stroll, The Bird, The Dirty Dog, as they listened to Chubby Checker, Little Eva, Smokey Robinson, Mitch Ryder and the Detroit Wheels, Junior Walker and a seemingly endless stream of one-hit wonders by whatever-happened-to artists. After a while, aided by the pole lamp, they even did The Limbo, when the girls' skirt-sense evaporated in *method champenoise* bubbles.

The models were all too young to have mastered these contortions with girlfriends on rainy afternoons to the sound of scratchy monaural 45's, but they seemed to be enjoying themselves in the slightly frantic, are-we-having-fun-yet? style of those who still think youth and beauty will turn life into a made-for-TV movie. The book was universally admired as a bit of classic retro chic, but I caught myself wondering if it wasn't easier to enjoy the past when you didn't have to claim it as your own.

At one point in the evening, it became apparent that several of the men, including Michael, were missing in action. I found them in my bedroom, watching my small colour portable Sony TV. When I cracked the door, they all looked sheepish, but I told them it was okay as long as they weren't watching sports or porn. Sports were strictly Sunday afternoon, not Saturday night, and porn was for fat balding losers, watching with bowls of Cheezies on their bellies, who'd later go to the STD clinic to see about the mysterious orange rash on their pricks.

I peered over the heads of Michael, an aspiring actor named Rex, Chris and Matthew's old friend Jack Morrison, who'd surprised me by showing up, though I assumed he came to my parties mostly for the pleasure it gave him to introduce himself to the assembled trendoids as a 'solid waste technician.' Unlike Matthew but like most writers, Jack had a straight job. He'd recently moved out of municipal garbage collection to another government job in the wastewater treatment department of the Greater Vancouver Regional District. Sometimes, when people asked him what he did, he told them he was a 'shit-disturber.' If that piqued their curiosity, he'd start in with graphic descriptions of wading through tanks of liquified faeces in hip-waders with a paddle to remove the used condoms and hypodermic needles which can jam the blades of the fans which churn the muck down to a fine slurry. As a final windup, he'd take the person's hand firmly in both of his.

"It's not so bad. If I last one more year, they'll give me gloves."

I immediately recognized the movie they were watching. *Waspworks*, the film made of Matthew's first novel. Once I understood their embarrassment, I reasurred them.

"It's okay, I've seen it before. Several times. Just remember, while you're in here, we girls are comparing your inseam measurements and the dimensions of Buzz, the Personal Massage Unit."

Waspworks brought Matthew acclaim from both science fiction fans and literary critics. It made us prosperous, if not exactly rich; eminent, if not quite established. It and Frank Steinberg moved us to Toronto. A Canadian director who'd paid his dues through the National Film Board shorts and low budget American-financed shlock horror movies shot in Canada for the tax breaks, Steinberg had acquired a reputation for bringing a cool perverse brilliance to the tackiest script.

When *Waspworks* began to sell significantly in the American lists, Steinberg contacted Matthew personally and pressured his own investors into ponying up a fair but reasonable price for the rights to a book that hadn't hit the U.S. best-seller charts yet. He admittted to Matthew he'd have to pay twice as much if the book did, an amount he couldn't afford without spending money he wanted to spend on the film. He loved *Waspworks*, he told Matthew, and was desperate to make the film, so his offer included an invitation to collaborate on the screenwriting for credit and a percentage. The arrangement printed money for them both.

Chris was rapt, more about Steinberg's film than about the novel written by his old friend, whose book-jacket photos were part of his own portfolio.

"Steinberg's a fucking genius...the cinematography..."

Jack Morrison shook his head.

"No, Matt always had an instinct for visual continuity. The linear narrative is just a sketch for the imagery. Memory, dream, fantasy and reality, seamlessly blended. Pure communication. All Steinberg had to do was shoot it as it was written."

I wasn't that fond of *Waspworks*. I'd typed the manuscript too many times. It was just a story about an anti-social boy, one of those geeky outcast loners everyone remembers going to school with, who goes into the woods alone to play solitary primitive games, killing birds and squirrels after trapping and torturing them. On one of his outings, he takes off his clothes and daubs himself with mud and crude paints, then begins drumming out an enigmatic message to the universe on a huge hollow log with two sticks, unaware that the log shelters an immense wasp nest. Thousands of wasps emerge and sting him almost to death. He's paralysed, like a stroke victim, as a result of the overdose of venom. Later, in the hospital, he discovers in his drugged dreams that he can communicate with and control the wasps. His will merges with the conglomerate insect will of the hive. Through the wasps, he attempts to communicate with his family, the community, his teachers and classmates and the one girl who has tried to befriend him. When the attempts are misunderstood and repulsed, he uses the wasps to destroy the town.

I found the scenes in which he attempts to initiate his girlfriend into his woodland mysteries quite erotic, since the girl undresses, obviously anticipating her first sexual experience, not some weird initiation into personal paganism, but I thought the rest of the story was predictable and grim. A plague of wasps descends on the town as he tries to deliver his message of peace and tranquillity through co-operation and unity of mind. The residents, armed with power-washers, welding rigs and gasoline instead of the traditional torches, finally attack the nest, led by the girl, and wipe it out. Barely enough wasps survive to infest the hospital and finish off their failed Messiah.

More than once, as Matthew pored over books on entomology, studying all the different types of wasps, I wondered aloud why he'd picked such a nasty creature, but he always had an answer for any question.

"The wasp is the perfect victim. It produces nothing except more wasps. No honey. To us, it's a pest. Yet it has a place in the scheme of things we don't appreciate. Vermin know more about the real balance of nature than we do. They fit in. They have a role. Rats, cockroaches, silverfish, wasps and flies. They reproach us because we don't understand them at all. We can't imagine why they exist, why they should be so much more perfect than we are. They seem like unnecessary sores on an otherwise quite nice planet, proof that God has too much time on his hands… Like human beings."

Matthew's second novel, *Channel Zero*, also made into a Frank Steinberg film, explored the possibilities of benign cancer. The story of a young girl this time, who becomes a kind of emotional radio transmitter between people she touches when she develops an unusual brain tumour. The sicker she gets, the more intense and wide-ranging her powers become, no longer dependent on touch to connect to people's thoughts and feelings. Politicians and religious leaders begin settling the most long-standing and blood-drenched conflicts as her influence grows and spreads. Prepared to die to save the world from itself, she is 'saved' by an experimental surgical procedure, a kind of brain-rape, performed by an international panel of doctors at the behest of political masters frightened by the prospect of world peace who want to preserve the political and economic status quo. It ends with the girl, her short term memory erased, in a suburban kitchen, now married to her accountant fiancée, making the small talk of married life, a parody of real communication.

Jack shrugged knowingly.

"In his head, Matt was always writing for film…"

Matthew and Jack had a falling out late one night years ago at a kitchen table at some stupid party where everyone was ankle-deep in broken glass and spilled wine. Imploding rock bands call this 'artistic differences' to disguise the fact that they're all just assholes, though in this case it was still pretty accurate. Jack was holding forth in a general way, accusing science fiction writers of using the genre to write popular entertainments with serious issues iced-on as topical hooks to add false intellectual weight to the product, so readers and film-goers could feel smug because they'd read or seen something 'important,' while the fantasy genre released them from an existential obligation to act on what they'd supposedly learned. Or something like that.

Euphoric with Glen Morangie and success, Matthew interpreted Jack's remarks as a veiled personal attack, which probably did have its roots in the fact Jack thought he was a better writer and envied Matthew's success. The debate ended in spilled whiskey, thrown glasses, mis-thrown punches and what reporters call 'a scuffle' as friends pulled them apart and Matthew landed his verbal knockout, something along the lines of "You're just jealous because I've had a novel published and it's going to be a film and you're going to be driving a cab until your head sinks down to your ass so you can shit out your mouth like you're doing now."

They hadn't spoken in ten years. Matthew was wrong about Jack driving a cab forever. He'd quit after one of the other cabbies was robbed and killed with a gun the killers swore in court they bought from another cab driver. The Mounties questioned Jack, but no charges were ever pressed and he'd never talked about it to anyone I knew. After a decade of travel and freelance writing, he hired on the North Vancouver District garbage trucks. Matthew couldn't help crowing, even though I could tell it hurt him to gloat over someone who had been a very close friend.

"He's gone from just talking garbage to actually tossing it for a living. Leave it to Jack to find a lower rung on the social ladder than pushing a hack."

Jack said picking up garbage inspired him to keep writing. His first collection of short stories all involved things that turn up in garbage cans, how they got there and what happens to them. When *Trashcan Babies* was published by Vancouver's Blacksmith Press, he sent us a copy, suitably inscribed, though he couldn't resist adding a couple of deliberately grimy fingerprints under the signature on the flyleaf. I thought Matthew would relent and at least send him a congratulatory note, if not call.

Instead, Matthew found out through Chris that Jack was working at a sewage treatment plant. Then he went down to the Ostomy Supply on St. Clair West, whose window display dummy was a kind of prosthetic mascot we called Bandage Man, and couriered Jack a colostomy-bag. I never saw him read *Trashcan Babies*, but I found the autographed, and finger-printed, book carefully tucked into the shelves in the study among all the other autographed copies he'd swapped with famous writers. Matthew was hedging his bet, but he could never get past the third scotch without taking up the argument and I had to stand in and take the verbal chain-whipping for Jack so many times it actually made me feel closer to him.

"Morrison is the worst kind of fuck-up on the planet, a writer who has talent and imagination but doesn't trust it. He has to go looking for *real* stories among *real* people. As if any of those morons out there in the street are *real*. All that Francois Villon and *Jean* Kerouac authenticity is great shit, until the real world rips out your guts and leaves you for dead in the street. Good luck making art out of some subhuman geek frisking you for your wallet while your life's blood is leaking into a storm sewer. The gutters are full of dead meat who thought they had to suffer every minute to produce these little shit-smears they call art…"

Matthew meant the other shooting Jack was involved in. When he was freelancing, Jack parlayed his familiarity with Vancouver's seedier streets into a couple of features that were picked up by Toronto magazines. They appealed to Torontonians who envied Vancouver's weather but were sick of its "jogging past the March daffodils in spandex and snacking on frozen tofu sherbet" superiority. They loved seeing the ugly underbelly of Lotus Land exposed while they were still wearing three layers of clothing.

He was on an assignment with a girl they both knew from high school. She'd been a call-girl for awhile, then became a model before learning to be a photographer. She actually gave me my first modelling contacts as a favour to Matthew. He had ten years to be grateful, but never got over his suspicions about my business because he knew her history. While on a photo-shoot near the Olympus Hotel, one of the old Welfare Wednesday hotels on the North Van waterfront, she and Jack were shot at by a sniper. She was killed. The sniper was never caught. Jack never talked about that either.

I always knew from the way Matthew ranted on about it that he wasn't just shocked at the idea of a *writer* being shot at, never mind a photographer being killed. Deep down, he saw her death as punishment for her life and liked bringing it up as a coded warning to me of the dangers of jumping the rails. Yet it was obvious he actually envied Jack in some weird way he could never admit. It made him smaller and he knew it and hated Jack for it.

Of all our friends from the old days, only Jack and Harry Lamb, a transplanted English punk rock bassist, made a point of calling and coming by when I left Matthew and came back to Vancouver. Both surprised me by not hitting on me, making drunken four a.m. confessions of long-smothered secret love and trying for a quick one with the ex of a friend. After years of drunken poverty, Harry had unexpectedly inherited a title and so much money from an uncle back in England it made his boyish attempts to be a black sheep wastrel ne'er-do-well musician seem absurd and he spent most of his time trying to live down his unearned wealth, while the boys mockingly called him Lord Harry.

"If you need anything, anything at all Eve, you only have to call."

He gave me the phone number of his castle, Umbridge Manor, which looked like a place you'd shoot a bad German horror movie about female vampires who all look like strippers from the 70's and get naked with their female victims for a bit of lesbian action before going for the jugular milkshake. Jack told me the same thing and gave me the number of his basement suite on Adanac Street in the downtown eastside.

The music was ending and so was the party. Wasps were stinging the paralyzed boy to death on the screen in the bedroom and the boys had lost interest and started doing the career one-up thing men do, so like locker room weenie measuring. After Rex detailed his latest triumphs in an Arts Club stage revue, his leading role in a fast food TV commercial, and his expectation of a call-back for a major supporting role in a made-for-TV movie of the week to be shot here for the tax breaks, Chris made a point of including Jack in the conversation by asking with sepulchral gravity how the novel he was known to be writing was coming along. As Rex eyed him with new respect, Jack took a pull on his beer.

"Like a dancer dosed with castor oil."

Rex leaned forward attentively. Actors are always interested in people who can put words into their mouths and make them seem interesting.

"What's it about? I mean, if you're one of those writers who refuses to talk about his work, I respect the creative process…"

"No, I don't mind. It's a picaresque tale of misadventure inspired by that old saying, 'Up Shit Creek without a paddle.' *Shit Creek* was the original working title, but lately I'm leaning toward *A River of Shit*. It has more tone, like *A River Runs Through It*, y'know? Hemingway said, 'write what you know' and I figure that since I know shit…'

I left them in it. The girls were in the kitchen being frank about their sex lives over the last of the wine. One of the models eyed the Personal Massage Unit reposing in it's long satin-lined box, ready to relieve the stress and tension of professional women at the touch of a button.

"Sometimes, after Brad's gone home to get his beauty sleep, I wish someone would give me a present like that."

Laine lit her last cigarette and proudly tossed the empty pack on the table into a welter of torn wrapping paper, chicken bones, dip-encrusted ramekins, empty glasses and ashtrays.

"Well, your house is properly warmed now."

In fact, I realized Michael and I would have at least an hour of clean-up to do before we could fall into bed safe in the knowledge we wouldn't have to wake up to a gag-making disaster in the morning. I had muffins, eggs, ham, and fresh cherries in the fridge, the French Roast Michael preferred in the coffee cannister.

Laine's announcement was the signal for a general retreat. Everyone fumbled for purses and coats, including Michael.

"I promised to drive Amanda home. Otherwise she couldn't have come. It's a long drive to Richmond and she's night-blind."

I gave him my best Client Smile.

"That was thoughtful of you. Should I pour you a cognac for a nightcap on your way back?"

He looked truly embarrassed, finally.

"Best not, I think. It's been a busy day. The party, the

long drive…"

I was glad we were alone in the kitchen at last.

"Yes. You'll be tired."

Nodding, he left in time to escort Amanda out with the crowd without being obvious, though I had the feeling everyone was deliberately not looking at me and acting drunker and more convivial that they felt. Amanda, at least, managed not to look obviously smug. When they were all gone, I went through the motions of tidying up, emptying ashtrays dishes and bottles into a large plastic garbage bag, settling the greasy dishes and glasses in hot water to soak, stowing soiled napkins in the laundry hamper and wiping down surfaces everywhere while I nibbled on a double brandy.

Only the presents got in the way, a clutter of unfamiliar things with no assigned place of their own. I kept moving them around, not knowing where to put them. Finally, I rooted around in the closet and found two large empty boxes left from when I moved in. I put everything that would fit into them and stacked the rest on top in a corner of the living room. Until I decided where to put them, at least they were out of the way

On the tea chest, nothing remained but *Swingin' Shindig*, the dances of the Sixties instruction book, the Personal Massage Unit and a roll of white pages, Lisa's story. I thumbed blankly through the book, wondering what had become of the models who posed for the pictures. Where were they were now? What expressions had their frozen grins of youthful joy turned into? I remembered rainy afternoons and sock-hops, girls dancing with each other because the boys were too cool or too shy, learning the complex steps of dances we thought would help us navigate the labyrinth of the future.

Putting down the book, I picked up the box and took out the Personal Massage Unit. It was long and thick, a surprisingly delicate shade of pink. Tentatively, I pressed the button countersunk in the handle. The room filled with a discreet hum, like the sound of a sleepy giant wasp. I snapped it off immediately, put it back in the box and tossed it onto the pile of presents in the corner as decisively as I tossed off the last of my brandy. Out of options, I poured another, the one that should have been Michael's, undid the black ribbon and unrolled the pages Lisa had given me.

Chapter 8

Stretched on the couch in the cocoon of light created by the glow of the lava-lamp Chris had given me, I took a huge swallow of brandy, lit one of my few remaining cigarettes and began to read Lisa's story. The title, *The Audience*, was hand written in some kind of glittery blue pen, though the text was Inkjet typed. Laine made sure Lisa was computer literate and always had the latest system upgrades because, as she put it, "In cyberspace no one can hear if you can't scream." There was no byline. As Lisa's note said, it was a story, a kind of fairy tale.

At last the poet was granted his long-awaited audience with the Emperor. Despite his rags and the snickers of the courtiers, he crossed the vast Audience Hall with immense dignity and knelt before the Throne, which was carved from an enormous block of ordinary stone and not decorated with gold or gems. Seated there, in a simple white robe, without a crown or sceptre, the wiz-

ened figure of the Emperor looked like a child taken to an adult party he didn't want to attend.

In the shadows to the Emperor's right stood his Treasurer, resplendent in golden robes. His face was hidden by an ornate mask of hammered gold. Around his neck he wore a thick gold chain from which hung the great golden key to the Imperial treasure house. To the Emperor's left, almost invisible in the shadow of the gigantic Throne, stood his Executioner. Swathed in a black cassock, his face was covered by a plain iron mask and his neck encircled by an iron chain, from which hung the iron key to the Imperial dungeons.

In a faint, quavering voice, The Emperor bade the poet rise and tell some tale of his own country and how he had come to be so far from home, seeking his bread among strangers. The poet bowed, paused for a moment, and began to speak in a voice that was resonant and commanding, not the voice of a beggar. Even the most arrogant and powerful courtiers, whispering behind fans and perfumed scarves, fell silent…

I took a deep drag on my cigarette and a deeper drag on the brandy. A bookish young girl showing off her precocious vocabulary. Matthew would have read this aloud for laughs, mocking the purple prose. He often wrote scathing critiques of this kind of work for the genre journals to which he occasionally contributed reviews in exchange for what he called his beer-money. But I couldn't stop reading. I wanted to hear what the poet said to the Emperor.

"In a distant land," said the poet, "There is a great range of mountains. It is impenetrable except for a single narrow pass. Long ago, there were two villages on the plains on either side of the mountains. All they knew of one another came from the tales of travellers who had survived the hazardous journey through the *pass. In both villages, the mountains were believed to be the home of the gods and such pilgrims were deeply respected. The travellers naturally exaggerated the wealth and generosity of the village from which they had come to appeal to the pride and hospitality of their hosts.*

"In time great kingdoms and empires arose in lands distant from the two villages and they began to communicate along the route which led through them and the mountains. The villages grew into trading posts and towns. They became great cities themselves, fabled places of clustered towers and shining domes girdled by walls of dressed stone…

What had this girl been reading? *The Arabian Nights*? More likely those pimply sword and sorcery pulps with their twee telepathic dragons. Or maybe she'd watched too many episodes of *Xena, Warrior Princess*. I touched up my brandy, leaving the bottle handy on the floor beside the couch and lit another cigarette off the butt of the last.

"Inevitably the rivalry between the two cities led to war. Poets invented the abduction of a Princess from one city by a Prince from the other because audiences love a tragic romance. Each hoping to catch the other by surprise, the cities gathered their armies and marched into the Mountains of the Gods. The savage tribes who lived in the mountains retired to their caves to watch and wait.

"The two armies met in the narrow pass. The generals of the armies were dismayed because their cavalry and siege weapons were useless, but they urged their soldiers to cover themselves with glory by capturing the pass. To inspire the men, the poets chanted odes to Victory to the rumble of drums and the shriek of flutes. The battle mounted in fury as the summer waned. The pass became a charnel-house. The stench of unburied bodies

fouled the mountain air and clouds of fat flies blotted out the sun. Sentries swore that at night they heard the clash of arms and eerie cries rising from the pass as the ghosts of the slain continued the terrible battle from dusk till dawn...

Shades of Poe had invaded the room. What time was it? Michael must have got Amanda home by now, surely. He should be crossing town in traffic light enough to enable him to use his cell phone without ramming a bus. Or to arrive momentarily. The intercom was silent as a tombstone. Shades of Poe, my ass.

"*One morning the soldiers awoke to find the carnage in the pass obliterated by a fine white shroud of snow. They constructed fortified camps and to these the armies retired, fighting only the wild mountain tribes who raided their supply convoys as they foundered in the deepening snow. In their drafty barracks the poets sang songs of the elegant cities they had left behind, of scented bowers and festival nights on delicate barges drifting on torchlit flowery canals.*

"*By spring, the armies were decimated by cold, starvation and despair and there was still no end to the battle. Both armies received reinforcements, but when they arrived the generals were dismayed to find they were the scum of the cities, penal battalions of cut-throats and thieves and beggars. Their officers were disgraced noblemen and bankrupt merchants whose families had bought their commissions to redeem their reputations.*

"*Neither army could advance and neither dared to retreat. In summer the soldiers hunted and fought battles like two great tribes. In winter they starved and froze. After a few years, men of the mountain tribes who desired to learn the arts of civilized warfare joined the armies and many of the soldiers imitated them by allowing their faces and bodies to be covered with fierce tattoos. Officers and men married women from the mountain tribes and the camps swarmed with their half-breed children. They learned to drink the powerful mead the mountain men brewed from wild honey and bitter herbs, forgetting the taste of the mellow wines of the cities. The poets traded songs with the rustic bards of the mountains and a harsh barbaric note enlivened their polished strophes…*

Strophes? What was a strophe anyway? I wasn't sure I knew or had ever known. Laine was right to be worried about Lisa if she was not only reading but writing this kind of shit. On the other hand, there were worse things a lovely girl her age could be doing, like imagining she was in love with some thirty-year-old biker who ran a speed lab. The line about the powerful mead made from wild honey and herbs made me thirsty and I tipped another inch of brandy into my glass.

"Many years passed before the generals were visited by dignitaries from their cities. Once, they were told, the two cities had been so rich and powerful they could resist even the great empires whose trading route they commanded. But years of war and the breaking off of trade had made them poor and weak and the great empires were impatient and threatening. A peace treaty was hastily negotiated, but the generals were told neither they nor their armies would be returning home immediately. The two cities still did not trust each other enough to leave the pass unguarded. They and their armies would remain as outposts and Wardens of the Pass. As the emissaries departed for the cities, the generals understood their long exile was only beginning…

"Despair settled over the camps like a cold, evil fog. The soldiers got drunk and armed themselves, as though preparing for battle, while their women and children cowered in the huts. The poets muffled their lyres for fear the discord of a misplayed note

or the twang of a breaking string might set off a massacre…

Twanging strings? Discords? Lisa had never heard a note of music in her life. And the cries and clashes of ghostly battles at night? Whatever she was reading, she was getting a lot more out of it than even Laine imagined. That last passage oddly reminded me of the atmosphere in our house in Toronto during the last worst days when Matthew and I exhausted the nights dredging up every cruel and inconsiderate thing either of us had ever done and throwing it in each other's faces, then spent the days tip-toeing around each other, murmuring monosyllables as if the house was booby-trapped, wired with terrorist bombs. But Lisa had been just a baby, too young to have any memory of her own parents' separation.

"The next morning, the generals of the two armies met alone, in secret, in the middle of the pass. By the time the mist had burned off, they returned to their armies and commanded their sullen troops to prepare to march. The forts and camps were put to the torch. As the flames rose behind them, the cheering soldiers, along with their native wives and children, began marching back toward the cities from which they had set out so long ago. As they passed through the mountains they were joined by troops of the tribesmen from the hills who had become their allies…

Well, at least somebody was going home. I wasn't. Not to Toronto anyway. It was never home. And not to Matthew anywhere. Once two people have said every soul-destroying thing they can say to one another, they can't just go back to making small talk over bagels and Blue Mountain coffee in the morning. I couldn't imagine how Matthew could stand to still live in the place, with the echoes of what I'd said to him and the things he'd been shocked to hear himself saying to me.

Was Michael home in his elegant understated West End studio? He should be, if he'd simply dropped Amanda at her door. I still half-expected a buzz on the intercom, the abashed admission he'd changed his mind halfway home. Men are usually incapable of passing up the slightest whiff of a fuck, no matter how ambivalent the circumstances. After Matthew and I had reduced each other to tears, exhaustion and malt whiskey numbness, we'd fall into bed and two minutes later his hand would be creeping up my thigh like a cat burglar trying to steal the Farewell Fuck Diamond. And just when I was feeling that I'd rather be gang-raped in a dumpster by homeless schizophrenics than ever endure his sly, tentative, opening-paragraph foreplay again.

And me? Was I finally home? My empty single bed waiting. A pot of coffee set for two I would drink myself. Despite the housewarming, the apartment still looked more like someone was moving out rather than in.

"By the time they reached the plains, the armies had become vast hordes. They ravaged the countryside to feed themselves. When they drew up within sight of the great cities they had almost forgotten, they were met by volunteer militias made up of their own sons, brothers, uncles, cousins and old friends. Battles were joined in which fathers slew sons who had been children when they went away to war, brother killed brother, friend cut down friend. Even the poets cast aside their lyres, drew their ornamental daggers and threw themselves into the fray, raving incoherently…

"The men of the cities fought desperately, but the men from the mountains were lean and irresistible as wolves. They stormed the massive walls and broke down the huge gates. The cities burst into flames behind them as they swept through the broad paved

streets. Shining domes and towers blackened and collapsed like burning flowers, toppling into the streets to crush defender and attacker alike. A hot poisonous rain of precious stones clattered on the bloody pavements, scorching those who tried to pick them up. Gold foil peeled away from statues like seared skin. Crystal fountains and canals were choked with gore. Men raped their own wives and daughters and cut their throats without recognizing them as they looted their own burning houses. In the twilight sky over the mountains, some paused long enough to see an immense pillar of smoke rising like a horrid monument from the other city on the plains beyond the Mountains of the Gods...

I had goosebumps and felt sick, though I told myself it was the brandy. My first thought was that I had to talk to Laine, to show her the story and tell her to get Lisa into counselling on Monday. Then I remembered Lisa had given me the story and waited until her mother had left the room to do it. We'd played our little game, Keep Mom Sweet, as co-conspirators and the story was my reward, a glimpse of the real Lisa, however filtered through the pulp fiction styles of two millennia. I couldn't tell Laine anything without betraying Lisa and doubly enraging Laine because I and not she had been its recipient, its audience.

"In the morning light dimmed by ashes, some of the tribesmen who had joined or followed the armies, along with some soldiers, fled away laden with plunder, back to their homes in the Mountains of the Gods. Others, with their concubines and children, began a degenerate existence among the smouldering ruins of the once great cities. Many more, led by the generals, marched on, away from the devastation to the borders of other states and empires, where they lived outcast lives of nomadic banditry, hunted and pursued into the waste places of the world. Farthest

of all wandered the poets, who travelled to the distant courts of Princes, Kings and Emperors, carrying this tale of their sufferings and of the two villages and the Mountains of the Gods…

I emptied the last two inches of brandy into my glass and lit my last cigarette. I knew enough about writers to know I was going to need both. I was tempted to just drop the pages in the wastebasket, click on Five-O in time to catch Jack Lord's shellacked hair defying the Trade Winds and hear the troubles of the world dismissed with a curt "Book him, Danno. Murder One." But I didn't.

There was silence in the vast Audience Hall. The Emperor had closed his eyes and seemed to be asleep. Not a courtier dared to cough. At last the Emperor opened his sad old eyes and looked once more upon the ragged poet.

"You shall be doubly rewarded," he said, raising his right hand.

The Emperor's Treasurer stepped forward. Light blazed off his golden mask and the great golden key upon his breast.

"See that he is well paid," said the Emperor.

Then the Emperor raised his left hand. The Imperial Executioner stepped from the shadows. His blank iron mask reflected no light at all.

"Cut out his tongue," said the Emperor.

Chapter 9

All week I studied the boxes in the corner of the living room over the rim of my brandy glass. Even neatly stacked out of the way, they dominated the room like the packed-up belongings of a murdered roommate. Matched crystal snifters were buried in there somewhere, but I didn't want to dig them out. Instead, I drank out of one of the large plain glass balloons I'd picked up cheap at London Drugs. They were big enough to rest comfortably in the palm, the stem dangling between fingers, and big glasses have the effect of making even a quad brandy look like just a splash.

The copy of *Swingin' Shindig* lay on the tea chest like an unconsulted *I Ching*. Beside it lay the story Lisa had given me, re-read every night before bed as if I expected it to have a different ending, but I was starting to forget what Jack Lord looked like and the TV was as cool as the fridge. I hadn't turned it on all week, not even to watch the news. By Saturday,

I hadn't heard from Michael and Laine was breaking in her new young man, Mark, a Shaughnessy boy with a trust fund from old money that owned a major Vancouver newspaper back when they were truly independent, not the trophy wives of social-climbing ad salesmen who wanted to see themselves described as 'press barons' in Macleans, or tentacles of some media conglomerate.

At university in the U.S. on a hockey scholarship, Mark Packer dabbled in publishing courses between backgammon, poker and hockey games and boinking compliant coeds. Lucky he did, since like a lot of young men who have the talent to be the next Wayne Gretzky, he suffered a chance knee injury in practice the year he should have made the U.S. Olympic team and been scouted by the National Hockey League. Since he'd neglected to fit much course work into his busy schedule that last semester, he decided publishing was in his blood after all and came to Vancouver.

With a wave of his cheque-book, he founded a magazine called *City Seen,* whose features originally consisted of inevitably effusive restaurant reviews and event listings, filled out by local entertainment, business and sports celebrities uttering likable lies about how the outrageous sums of money they were paid for their questionable talents weren't nearly as personally satisfying to them as shilling for trendy charities raising money for victims whose diseases or conditions prevented any of them from attending these events and turning them into freak shows.

Jack Morrison wrote a few articles for the magazine, when he'd been blacklisted by every other editor in the city for his habit of delivering caustic, highly fanciful email replies to queries about why his copy was late, likely to offend advertisers or incoherent. Initially, Mark said, he'd liked Jack's pieces on the lesser known and meaner streets of Vancouver because they gave the magazine 'edge.' His enthusiasm faded after the assignment which resulted in the shooting of the photographer outside a tough North Vancouver waterfront bar.

As a result of the incident and his reputation as a 'loose cannon' among editors on the local scene, Jack vanished for a few years, ironically emerging as one of those journalists who report from places the government has issued travel warnings against. Collections of his articles, *Newspaper Shoes, Bullets & Champagne* and *Neutron Blonde,* appeared in his absence. I'd see them in bookstores on Queen Street and sneak them home in my purse, reading them on the big red rocket Toronto streetcars or the subway. He never sent copies of these books to Matthew, knowing his opinion of journalism. Then, a year or so before I left Matthew, I heard Jack had suddenly turned up in Vancouver again and got a job with the North Van City Works, then the Greater Vancouver Regional District, claiming he needed a steady paycheque because he'd rather starve and write fiction than ever write another word of journalism.

Laine met Mark when Justin, his advertising manager, an odious little reptile who decked himself in cheap Moore's Tailors suits, began hiring models from The Agency as window dressing for the celebs in their features and seasonal fashion spreads. It quickly became obvious, as the models adamantly refused repeat gigs, that this underdone weenie was attempting to use The Agency as an escort service, the way certain businessmen routinely use office temp services to recruit fresh talent for the after-hours 'cock-tales' circuit. At Laine's instigation, Justin was lately given a push down a long flight of berber-carpeted stairs and she took over as uncredited de facto fashion editor and consultant.

So now Laine had to "spend time with Mark" because he was once again stressed out over mistakes in ads and listings by the entry-level help he hired straight out of college journalism courses to do the grunt work and keep costs down. Laine had virtually demanded Chris Newman volunteer to boost the style and profile of *City Seen* with his photography, which involved trying to make community tabloid snaps of dime celebrities and gossip columnists posing on golf courses and the Whistler-Blackcomb ski slopes look stylish.

At my party, Jack politely declined Mark's suggestion that he pitch the magazine a few ideas for feature articles, saying he doubted *City Seen*'s readers would be interested in a detailed description of what happened to their low-fat lattes, biscotta, bruschetta, Pad Thai and sushi, along with their abundant condoms and tampons, after they flushed. Resentful at being sent on assignments like a pool photographer, Chris treated Mark as if he'd just announced he was HIV-positive and persistently referred to the magazine as Shitty Scene. This provoked Laine to snappishly remind him how rare and fortunate he was among photographers to be so highly paid for his work for The Agency, he could afford to bring his creative genius to bear to help a struggling publication and at the same time repay certain unspecified debts of gratitude for the lifestyle he currently enjoyed.

Laine's defense of her relationship with Mark was unusually frank.

"He has trust fund capital he can't piss away…and he owns a magazine, which we, at The Agency, can improve to our mutual advantage, if we all work together." By this, she meant junior clients could expect to be on-call to turn up at events *City Seen* would be covering and add their polish, beauty and glamour to the festivities, which Chris would capture on film and Mark's staff immortalize in suitably gushing cutlines.

In his late thirties, Mark was slightly outside Laine's target profile, but like everyone else, she wasn't getting any younger. How much longer would she be able to attract men from her preferred age-group? This one had good connections and old money he couldn't squander. He also had a magazine which could be improved by drawing on a talent-pool she controlled, drawn into her wide personal web and re-shaped into an launch platform for the careers of clients of The Agency. If it all seemed a bit cooly calculated, well, I was hardly in a position to argue the case for True Love, under the circumstances.

With Laine occupied applying the kind of balm to Mark's ego no mere banker can confect, under the duress of a dateless weekend, I finally succumbed and clicked on the TV. One of the local stations was holding a Frank Steinberg film festival on the Late Movie and I tried to watch a re-run of *Channel Zero*, but fell asleep after the second reel and most of a bottle of brandy.

Sunday morning I woke up on top of the bed, alone and fully dressed, with Lisa's story in my hand, a mouth like an industrial spin-dryer, a head like a hit-and-run victim and a preacher shaking and ranting at spastics on the overheated TV, commanding them to rise and walk. It was a stunningly sunny day and my hangover was one of the manic ones that wouldn't let me escape into sleep, one of those serve-you-right-to-suffer hangovers that threatened to compel me to dust, vacuum, wash walls, rearrange non-existent furniture and clean out the fridge, to mortify the spirit and the flesh with work.

By the time I showered, brushed my teeth for the third or fourth time, drank a quart of orange juice and a cup of coffee, I knew I couldn't stay in the apartment a minute longer. While my brain was still incapable of rational thought, I carried the two boxes of housewarming presents one at a time down to the parking lot and loaded them into the Mini's small back seat. The *flambé* set alone took up most of a whole box and I had to make an extra trip with an armload of things to pile on top.

Seeing me burdened in the hall, one of my neighbours held the door to the stairs open for me. He did not, however, offer to relieve me of any part of my burden, the fat-assed balding bearded lump with the sly look of the chronic peeper and wanker around his eyes. Clutching his morning *Province* against his chest like a shield, he wasn't too timid to ask, "Moving out?" Obviously had a list of fellow self-fondlers looking for the faintest hint of an inside track to get into the building. It occurred to me there must be whole buildings of tasteful bachelor apartments inhabited by these suety inverts, who do some anonymous job all day during the week, then return to their womb-like cells, their enveloping couches prostrate before sixty-inch plasma tv screens, to nibble spring rolls, pizza and Cheetos as they search the internet with high-speed modems and pentium power, seeking images of some aspect of human sexuality so impossibly, so unthinkably degrading, it will make them feel like morally superior beings just for not having thought of it.

Moving hadn't actually occurred to me, but I answered on a whim.

"I'll let you know."

By the time I rammed the pole-lamp in diagonally with the fixture out the passenger window, there was just enough room for me to drive if I stayed in third gear all the way. Unable to face the makeup mirror, I tied my hair back with an elastic and put on a pair of cheap sunglasses I couldn't remember buying. With the copy of *Swingin' Shindig* in my shoulder bag, I drove across town, the Mini sagging on its shocks, its tranny whining miserably, to the Terminal Avenue Flea Market. Offering my wrist to the Sikh at the door like a supplicant, I entered the immense shadowy interior of the building as gratefully as a convert visiting a venerable cathedral.

He wasn't at the same table. There was a different man there, older, with Slavic features, hostile because I showed no interest in his wooden plaques decorated with decoupage of horse heads and western scenes. When I asked about the man with the books and tapes, he shrugged and ignored me, almost driving me to panic. Then, as I peered desperately around at the thickening crowd of bargain-hunters, collectors and looky-lous, I saw him several tables away on the other side of the aisle. He was bent over, studying the liner notes of an old record jacket.

"I thought you might like to have this back."

I laid the copy of *Swingin' Shindig* on the table in front of him, an offering. He didn't seem surprised to see me. He didn't smile, but recognized me with a nod, though I must've looked nothing like the Bitch Sidekick he remembered.

"Uh, thank you... Thank you very much."

"Your Elvis isn't half bad... It's awful."

He smiled then. It occurred to me that in spite of the

calm, stubborn aggression he'd displayed in his encounter with Laine, he was actually a bit shy. I looked at him with a helplessness I hardly had to fake.

"Could you do me a really big favour?"

"Since you've done me one? The book, I mean."

"I have some things outside in the parking lot. In my car. I wondered if you could look at them and maybe… I don't know… I don't know anyone who does this kind of…who deals in things, you know?"

He hesitated, obviously trying to imagine what trash I might have in the car and how he could politely tell me to fuck off. In the end, he opted for the path of least resistance.

"Sure, well, I guess I could look at them… Willie will watch my table, won't you Willie?"

An ancient man with the toothless chronic smile of the permanently bewildered nodded from behind a display of shoes that looked like they'd collectively walked around the planet two or three times. I followed the man toward the door while he talked nervously over his shoulder.

"Willie's got a thing about shoes. He used to be a shoe-maker, back in the Old Country, wherever that is, before they were all made by drones at machines. Now all shoe-makers do is try to patch shoes that aren't worth fixing because they weren't worth making in the first place. It's because we use cars to get around. We don't walk the way people did in Europe in his day, so we don't need the kind of crafted durable shoes they did. Willie can't see it. Doesn't understand why even our hiking boots, those fancy rugged looking 'trail shoes,' are really just faked up versions of cheap laminated sneakers because people only wear them a couple of times a year. He can't understand a country where good shoes aren't important and where people have so many bad shoes. At least, I think that's what he says. He doesn't talk much and when he does a lot of what he says isn't English. I'm not sure if it's really any language at all or just one he makes up…"

In the parking lot, I opened the stuffed Mini, but the car was so small he had to pull the boxes out to look at them. I was more embarrassed than I expected, like a well-to-do woman in a pawnshop. People who'd just parked their cars, who hadn't even gone into the flea market, as well as some who'd obviously already been from the look of the unlikely stuff they were carrying, came over to stare at my things without a trace of tact or shame. He held up a glass, flicking the rim with a fingernail to produce a clear ringing note audible even over the grumble of traffic on Terminal Avenue.

"This is crystal. This stuff is all brand new. I can't buy it off you. I can't give you anything like what it's worth. You could get the full value just by returning it to the stores. Have you got the receipts?"

Exasperated, I shook my head.

"I don't want to return it. I really just want to get rid of it. All of it. Now."

A plump woman nudged her husband as she peered around his shoulder. She wore very tight stretch pants, which made me think of Chris, who was always threatening to publish a coffee-table book of photographs titled *Women Who Shouldn't Wear Spandex.*

"Honey, ask him how much for those glasses."

The woman's husband tugged at the bill of his Canucks baseball cap.

"I'll give you ten bucks for those four glasses, man."

He had a gruff take-charge voice. My companion rounded on him indignantly, his manner suddenly reminding me of his run-in with Laine. "Ten bucks? Don't make me laugh in your face. These glasses are the finest European crystal. Brand new. Still in the wrappers. Never been drunk out of, never mind slobbered in. They cost at least fifteen bucks. Each. That's sixty bucks worth of beer glasses you're looking at, bud. You'd have to start drinking Heineken just to live up to them."

"Okay, well…fifteen then."

My new friend shook his head.

"Double it, I'd still be giving you a deal below fifty percent of their retail. Where was the last place you saw crystal like this on sale for even twenty percent off? Not at The Bay, man, and sure as shit not at your local Zellers."

The plump woman nudged her husband and began to whine in his ear.

"He's right, honey, and they'd look just perfect in my china cabinet…"

The Canucks man shushed her with a look.

"Okay, twenty…and that's my last offer."

The small crowd was enjoying itself. If the Mini had been bigger, I'd have crawled under it. A well-dressed young woman in the crowd got into the act, ignoring her boyfriend's reflexive look of panic.

"Shit, I'll give you thirty for them right now."

The plump woman gave her a look that would freeze the blood of a plague rat. My self-appointed agent shrugged at his opponent in the Canucks cap.

"There. You see? And at thirty, I can't even take a commission. These glasses retail for fifteen or twenty *each*, for Christ sake…"

The man in the Canucks cap was getting pissed off. His fat wife kept pinching him and he looked like he might be about to return the favour with more than two fingers.

"You're not supposed to be selling stuff out in the street, anyway. You need a license for that. You're supposed to be inside…"

My man smiled quietly.

"Inside, they're forty, ten bucks each, and no dickering. Now, do you want them or do I deal with the young lady over here?"

"Honeeee…"

"Okay, okay. Thirty-five. That's it."

The man pulled out a long truckers' wallet connected to his wide belt with a short length of chain. The plump woman bounded on the toes of her Nikes, squealing triumphantly. At the last moment my agent seemed to remember these things were not his to sell. He shot me a frantic, "Is that alright with you?" look. I nodded quickly. As the plump woman marched away, the box of crystal glasses cradled between her generous breasts, grumbling husband trailing in her wake, my friend handed me thirty-five dollars. I shook my head.

"I'll split it with you. After all, you did the selling…"

"No. You keep it. That guy was right. I don't have any right to sell this stuff on the street. Like I said, I can't afford to buy this stuff from you, but if you really want to get rid of it, if you don't want to take it back to the stores, I'll help you sell it inside…You can use my table. I didn't bring much this week. Just came to look around and hang out…"

"Are you sure? I don't know anything about…"

"Okay. If it makes you feel better, I'll take ten percent for the table, as a consulting fee." He smiled at me for the first time. "Besides, this stuff will attract more people to the table. I usually only get collectors."

He seemed to be making some distinction between himself and a mere junk dealer, but I was too relieved to read the sub-titles. Carrying one box while he carried the other, the pole lamp braced under one of his arms like Lancelot escorting the Queen, I felt myself crossing an invisible border, an unseen line drawn across the grimy threshold of the old building. I still felt uncomfortable as we unpacked the boxes and laid the presents out on his table. What if Laine turned up with Mark? Or one of the models and her boyfriend? Then I noticed he was opening the box containing the Personal Massage Unit. My hand flew to my mouth.

"Oh my God… I forgot that was in there. That was a gift…a joke, I mean. It's never…"

"Been used?"

He finished my gaffe for me with a snort of laughter. Willie gave me a toothless grin, gabbling with mercifully incomprehensible enthusiasm.

"We can't put that out."

He chuckled.

"You bet we can. And I'll bet you a coffee it's the first thing we sell and we get top dollar for it. I mean, who's going to stand here and haggle over it?" He placed it prominently at first, then after consideration withdrew it to a more discreet corner of the table. "Don't want to scare off the squeamish types who might buy the other stuff."

It wasn't the first thing we sold, but it did sell. A slim spinsterish type with hennaed hair, who looked like a librarian or legal secretary shopping for antiques or discount books, picked up the box and opened it as she perused our display.

Blushing furiously, she shut the box at once and dropped it as though it contained a live snake. Nervously adjusting her own suddenly necessary dark glasses, she peered briefly at me with frank curiosity, then at my new friend, who smiled as she drifted away.

"She'll be back."

"How do you know?… I mean, you didn't seem surprised when I came back, but you don't know anything about me… And I don't even know your name."

"People just call me Buzz."

I nearly wet my pants laughing. When I got my breath back and explained why, it was his turn to laugh. He eyed the other Buzz, a.k.a. Bob, the Battery-Operated Boyfriend, with mock awe.

"Don't think I measure up, in size or endurance…But I do have No Batteries Required stamped on my ass."

"So why do they call you Buzz?"

"Because I prefer it to the name I used to have."

"Okay, Buzz."

I didn't ask what his real name was or why he didn't like it. If he didn't want it, it seemed fair enough to discard it in this place where all sorts of things nobody wanted were being traded and sold. I'd told him my real name and realized I'd missed an opportunity, maybe the only one I'd ever get, to invent an alias, to just become someone else, take on another identity without the formality of the Change of Name Act, like someone on the run whose picture on Wanted posters boasts the letters a.k.a, also known as, before a dozen imaginary identities. I wished I'd thought faster. I could have been Natasha, Marlene, Desiree. No, they sounded too much like strippers stage names. On the other hand, neither he nor Willie nor anyone else at the flea market knew I wasn't an exotic dancer on the skids. I might be anything, anyone. Buzz was right about the woman. She came back while I was alone, minding the table while he went to get a couple of Cokes and cigarettes for me. She materialized out of the crowd in front of me, nervous as a vampire at noon.

"How much is this?"

Her voice was a tense whisper. She still wore her dark glasses in spite of the dimness. My only experience of haggling had been watching Buzz in the parking lot and at the table. Matthew always habitually shopped around to get the best price on major purchases, but people with Gold Visa cards do not haggle. I wanted to say, "Take it. It's yours," but somehow I knew that would insult her, implying some pathetic need. She wanted to pay.

"Ten bucks… Tax and batteries included."

I heard myself saying it, but hardly recognized my own voice. Instinctively I rounded it to an all-inclusive price, sensing she wouldn't want to stand there holding it while I struggled to make change. Instantly a ten-spot appeared in my hand and the Personal Massage Unit vanished into the woman's large bag. Almost as quickly, she was gone, lost in the crowd again. Buzz returned with the Cokes and smokes.

"If you're going to smoke, I can get them for you a lot cheaper through a friend who brings them in from Alberta." Then he noticed the empty spot on the table. "She came back."

"How d'you know it was her?"

He grinned. "I saw her lighting out with a bulge in her bag in a big hurry, like she wanted to get home and see if it matched the drapes. She laid rubber out of the parking lot and that's some trick in a Ford Escort."

By five o'clock we'd sold everything I'd brought as well as some of his tapes, books and records. I noticed he put the copy of *Swingin' Shindig* into his knapsack, though, not back on the table. Despite the knock-down prices, I had over six hundred dollars in my purse, less his ten percent.

Chapter 10

All week, I eyeballed every remaining object in the apartment, calculating frequency of usage, general utility, aesthetic merits, mercilessly re-evaluating my remaining possessions. Even my walk-in closet was subjected to a surprise inspection parade. By Friday evening, I admitted to myself I was only looking for an excuse to go back to the flea market.

But it was more than that. The Sunday before, as Buzz and I sold off the last of the house-warming presents to a young couple who were thrilled to get such a deal on a set of designer sheets and pillowcases for their young daughter's first single bed, I experienced a feeling of relief, of lightness and liberation, more intense than anything I felt when I left the oppressive house in Toronto. I hadn't had so much fun since I learned to masturbate.

Not even another letter from Matthew's lawyer, urging

me to sign and return the Separation Agreement, properly witnessed, dangling bait in the form of a promise that my household furnishings were being carefully stored and would be shipped to my specified point of delivery upon receipt of the agreement, could take the edge off my buzz. A week before, the letter would have dropped me like a contract murder victim with an anklet of breeze blocks into the Slough of Despond. Now I simply tucked it back in the envelope and put it on my bedside table, under Lisa's story, which I still read every night before turning off the lamp.

Vicariously I savoured the power of the Emperor each night, the power to silence unwelcome news with a single command, the immense luxury of enforcing muteness on those who dared say anything you didn't want to hear, heedless of truth. I imagined myself on an immense cold stone throne, my nakedness masked only by a loose veil of jewels so dazzling in the torchlight no courtier could afterwards recall a single feature of my body, only that I had been incomparably beautiful as I ordered my muscular robed minions to go forth and tear out the tongues and cut off the fingers of certain writers and their lawyers, men who foolishly thought words had real power and could be used like weapons to hurt or intimidate.

The letter had the opposite effect intended. Instead of coveting my own possessions, I found myself trying to remember exactly what was there and estimating what I could get at the flea market for the lot, less ten percent. My first full day at the market had left me wrung out, wired up on too much silex coffee, my throat raw from smoking, but that night I slept better than I had in months, without brandy, without Steve McGarrett and without Michael, from whom I hadn't had so much as a recorded sigh all week.

Late Friday night, I phoned Buzz at the number he'd given me on the back of a grubby card from a defunct Chinese restaurant called The Jasmine Inn in North Vancouver. As I listened to the rings, I wondered if I'd get an answering machine, if he'd want one, what he could get for a used one like mine. Everyone I knew had a machine, each with its own cute personalized message, written, directed and performed by the owner. Actors auditioned on their machines. Musicians composed and played cute jingles on theirs. Writers read excerpts from their unpublished works. All of which no doubt resulted in a large number of no-message hang-up calls and ultimately defeated the purpose of the machines. Mind you, if their answering machine performances were anything to go by, a captive audience is better than no audience at all.

After too many rings, Buzz finally answered, out of breath and apologetic.

"Sorry. Couldn't find the phone. Do you know what it's like to hear the phone ringing and not be able to find it? Who are you and what do you want?"

"Buzz? It's Eve. From the flea market last week?" I hated my voice for making it sound like we'd met in some trendy bar and he might not remember buying me a Cran-Tini. "I've got a few more things I might want to get rid of and…"

"Oh, hi… Sure, well, of course… I mean, if you… I was going to go to the big swap meet at Cloverdale first thing, but…"

"That's okay. I know where it is. I could meet you there."

"Or I could pick you up. In the van, I mean. If you have stuff, that would be easier for you, wouldn't it? Your car's pretty small. I don't mind, but I leave early."

"I'll set my alarm. If you drive, I buy breakfast. That a deal?"

"Yeah? Okay." He sounded almost shocked. "I know this place in Cloverdale where you can still get bacon and eggs for two seventy-five…"

I set the clock radio alarm for an hour before the appointed time, wondering for a second how much that little deluxe digital unit would bring over the table. Ignoring the brandy bottle, I unplugged the TV before I turned in, unthreading the cable connection purposefully, as though strangling a small but poisonous snake. Purveyor of bad movies, inane talk shows, idiot infomercials, decades-old reruns, the bachelor and bachelorettes friend, the thing you turned on just for company, for the sound of a human voice when you came home to an empty apartment, it was going to Cloverdale tomorrow. The *TV Guide* advertised another installment of the Frank Steinberg Film Festival. I folded it neatly and put it in the garbage bin under the sink.

I was up, dressed and coffeed when Buzz arrived. The wicker basket by the door was filled with fashion magazines, the TV, a set of professional kitchen knives, six Swedish steel steak knives I'd forgotten I had, bone china cups and saucers Laine had given me and I'd never liked. As well, there were several black plastic garbage bags filled with clothes and shoes from the walk-in closet.

"What do you think?"

He nervously accepted a cup of Michael's French Roast and seemed glad to have the pile of things to look over.

"It's great stuff. But are you sure you want to get rid of it this way? I mean, you could get a lot more for these clothes at a consignment boutique in Kerrisdale or West Van. Pretty high end rags for a swap meet."

"I'd rather do it this way. Really."

He shrugged.

"Okay. Let's get it out to the truck and get on the road."

We drove to Cloverdale in his ancient blue Econoline. He told me he'd camperized it himself with odds and ends of carpet, old cabinets adapted to fit the corners, even a small sink with a bar fridge underneath and a foam mattress on a platform across the back, all from flea markets. It was tackier than fresh paint, a throwback to the 70's, but it had a homey, comfortable feel to it. He'd installed high-backed Captain's chairs in front, salvaged from the wreck of some RV dinosaur, and there were gimballed holders for beer cans or coffee cups fitted to the dash he'd taken from the same tragic vacation vehicle. A CB radio, tape player and radar detector were bracketed above the sun-visors, both of which sported vinyl sleeves with pockets for pens, combs, and a small mirror. A combination litter bag and map-holder saddled the console.

"I can live in this van. I actually did live in it all one year, in downtown Vancouver, without paying one cent in rent, though I got a few parking tickets. I had dozens of streets I used to park on at night. Streets are a lot safer than parking lots or parks. You get a lot of freaks in parks at night. I used to stop someplace until I got bored with the view. I lived in Shaughnessy, Kits, Point Grey, the British Properties. Great view, but the cops are like crab-lice. Rich peoples' Rent-A-Guards, protecting property and its owners. Not enough real crime to keep them slim, so they'll run your plate numbers through the computer just to see what you're doing in the neighbourhood, if they have time between visits to the donut shop…"

The weather was better than on my visit with Laine. That seemed an eon ago, when fierce dinosaurs walked the earth. There were more sellers and many more buyers and browsers already there, in spite of the hour. We were lucky to get a spot near the back of the open area by the buildings. If Buzz was disappointed, he didn't show it.

"Actually, this is better." We unpacked quickly onto the weatherbeaten table. "If you're too near the entrance, you only get impulse buyers. Real buyers hang onto their wallets until they've had a good look at everything and found what they want. If somebody comes back to your table twice, they're a probable. Three times, you can name your price."

After less than an hour behind the table, I felt like a kid who'd run away and joined the carnival. Customers and curiosity seekers shuffled up and down the aisles between the ragged rectangles of vans, trucks, and tables. Inside the enclosures of vehicles and tables, sellers swapped and gossiped, smoked over coffee, tea and the occasional furtive shot of whisky to keep off morning chill. It was like a gypsy camp, dominated by a *lingua franca* of offers, counter-offers and deals as mysterious as Romany or Shelta to the uninitiated ear. As I listened, sipping coffee from one of Buzz's Thermos jugs, I began to be aware of cross-currents of rivalry, jealousy, friendship and solidarity among the dealers, like an anthropologist getting her first glimpse of the inner life of a strange tribe.

Several dealers smiled or nodded to me, not only when they dropped by to talk to Buzz, but when I wandered among the crowd to stretch my legs. As in any small closed society, word got around quick. When the woman at the next table borrowed a smoke from me, then refilled my coffee mug from her own Thermos, adding a drop of sweet apricot brandy with a wink, then introduced me to another dealer as "Buzzy's partner," I felt I'd been accepted, adopted into the clan.

I found I preferred to stay within the enclosure, among the other dealers, or behind the table, listening to Buzz work the crowd. I thought he drove a harder bargain over my things, especially with two young women who reminded me uncomfortably of Laine and I slumming the flea market in hundred dollar sunglasses. They wound up buying several of my castoff outfits each, paying more, I suspected, than they would've in a suburban consignment store. For a guy whose wardrobe seemed to consist of WWII surplus, Buzz displayed a surprising knowledge of women's clothing labels. As the two marched off, clutching their purchases protectively, I shyly suggested he ease up a little on the haggling.

"You don't have to get top dollar, Buzz. The money isn't that important."

He gave me a stern look.

"Of course it is. Look, if people think they've got a bargain, then buying something makes them happy and they're happy with what they've bought, even though it may not be perfect. But if you just give something away, no matter how valuable it is, people assume it must be a piece of junk. Or else they feel like it's a gift and then they expect it to be perfect or it's an insult."

I was still thinking that over when I saw the black dog again. Head down, tongue trailing, it darted through the crowd and under our table, cowering behind my legs. In its wake, the mob parted for the burly chain-swinging form of the dog's owner. Dragging the dog from its refuge, he continued to curse steadily in his incomprehensible language as he beat the dog with the flying chain, oblivious to my overturned chair, spilled coffee and single sharp scream.

Buzz jumped over the table, shouting and dodging, fists raised.

"Drop that fucking chain, asshole, or I'll wrap it around your fat neck!"

The man paid no attention, dragging the whimpering dog away into the crowd. The woman at the next table spat after him.

"Gutless tub a shit…"

I climbed into the van and sat on the makeshift bed in the back, willing myself not to cry. Buzz came in a minute later.

"You alright?"

"No! I'm not all-fucking-right! Why doesn't somebody stop him doing that?"

My voice broke, betraying me. I lit a cigarette, almost breaking it, and puffed furiously.

"I know… He's an asshole… But it's his dog…"

"Well, he shouldn't be allowed to have a dog! Somebody should call the SPCA! Or do…something!"

I looked away, forcing myself to smoke, rubbing my marginal mascara carelessly on the back of my sleeve, trying to understand why I was suddenly so hurt and angry over one small act of cruelty among the legion of atrocities, brutalities and indifferences, sins of commission and omission, enacted in the world each and every second of each and every day.

"Keep an eye on the table."

When I looked around, he was gone. When I stepped out of the van, I noticed my portable Sony colour TV was gone as well. The woman next door offered me a medicinal shot of fruit brandy. I tossed it back and accepted another. The older woman shook her head, glancing at the spot where the TV had been.

"Buzz took it with him… That other rotted prick, if I was a man, I'd take that chain to his lard ass, then strangle him with it. Slowly."

Buzz was gone almost half an hour. When he returned, he wasn't carrying the TV set. The black Lab, unleashed or chained, followed him wearing that expression of absolute devotion which puts fickle human love to shame. Buzz gestured to the dog to go to me. Sitting beside my chair, it dropped its big black head in my lap and and sighed. I stroked the dusty head and velvety ears. The dog's dark brown eyes slowly closed.

"Thank you."

Buzz shook his head dismissively.

"Worst deal I ever made. A five-hundred-buck TV for a mutt who probably needs fifty bucks worth of shots, deworming, a twenty buck license, ten bucks worth of flea shampoo…"

"I don't care what it costs…"

"That's good, because he probably eats more than you do, too, by the look of you…"

"Buzz? I don't think I'm allowed to keep a dog in my apartment. I'll pay for all those things, his food, vet bills, everything, if…"

Buzz shut his own eyes and sighed.

"I guess I could use a watchdog around the shop. There's been break-ins in the neighbourhood since nineteen twenty-five."

I leaned over and put my arms around his neck, feeling him stiffen in surprise, then gradually relax. He put one awkward arm around me, his voice suddenly weary.

"It won't make any difference, you know. That fat fuck will just go out and get another dog to beat. You can't save all the dogs in the world…"

I raised my head.

"I know… I don't care. Don't tell me that now."

"What do you want to call him?"

The woman at the next table produced her liqueur bottle again.

"Call him Lucky, 'cause this is the luckiest day of his life."

I turned my chair away from the table. I'd started to cry again and I didn't know why, which made it worse, but I knew I wasn't just crying out of gratitude or relief or sadness at the plight of abused animals. Some log-jam even Dr. Stern hadn't been able to budge was breaking up at last in a flood that wasn't anything like the hot acid weeping of anger that had been trashing my makeup for months, but seemed to come straight from some unknown spring of grief deeper than the bottomless lakes of Siberia and the darkest trenches of the oceans. Thumping his tail against the gravel, Lucky the big black dog sat between my knees, his rough warm pink tongue patiently licking away the tears as they rolled down my cheeks.

Chapter 11

The shop was a narrow storefront on the steep slope of lower Lonsdale Avenue in North Vancouver. Harry's New-To-U in chipped fading brush script flowed across a grimy front window displaying used tools dangling from lengths of wire and chain, reminding me of instruments of torture in the faux-dungeon of a third-rate wax museum. Buzz unlocked the door and let Lucky bound in ahead to sniff around the perimeters of his new home.

"Hope he doesn't piss in the corners to mark his territory. Bad enough me doing it." He laughed at my sudden hesitation on the threshold. "Kidding… I'm housebroken, pretty much anyway."

To cover my embarrassment, I changed the subject.

"It seems kind of sad, I mean, all these tools with nobody using them. When you think of all the things they've probably built or fixed…and all the things that still need building and fixing in the world…"

I wondered if he'd laugh at me, but he didn't. As he ushered me into the musty dimness, there was a soft click behind me and the long room was flash-flooded with hard white fluorescent light. A single narrow aisle wound erratically to the curtained doorway of a back room. The aisle was barely that, almost impassable, crowded on both sides by furniture stacked on furniture, all of it piled with small appliances, knicknacks, assorted crockery, old magazines and newspapers. All but invisible, the walls were buttressed by makeshift bookshelves sagging under the weight of double rows of books and paperbacks, every bit of space in between hung with murky amateurish oils, fading prints and engravings, framed documents and diplomas from unlikely schools, photographs of strangers, all further obscured by racks and hooks from which hung bicycles, skates, skis, unstrung bows and stringless guitars, mandolins and banjos, lengths of decorative moulding, old pipe of various designs and dimensions and sets of mismatched luggage.

"I know what you mean. Sometimes, I feel like this is the asshole of the industrial world, the cloaca of capitalism. Last stop before the great landfill. Makes me feel a bit like a necrophiliac. Most of this stuff belonged to people who are dead now. It got handed down and stored in basements by kids who were grown up and had new things of their own until they forgot what it was supposed to mean or stopped caring. Then it wound up here, one stop short of the dump. A lot of things only need a little fixing and I've discovered I'm kind of handy at it. Then they're not just good as new, but usually better than what's sold new these days. You fix an old toaster from the Forties, it's going to be making toast for another sixty years, but when a toaster you bought last year goes on the fritz, you either can't fix it or it isn't worth fixing, like the shoes Willie's always on about. Just cheap junk inside. Even though I managed to get a lot of this old stuff working again, sometimes, when I'm sitting in here late at night with the lights off, this place reminds me of the pictures of ancient tombs in Egypt. The Egyptians might've been onto something when they used to bury a persons stuff with them. Maybe it was their version of planned obsolescence."

Gingerly I negotiated the congested aisle and followed him through the curtain into the back room where Lucky was waiting, having already taken possession of an overstuffed armchair. Buzz addressed him with mock severity.

"Okay. Let's get this straight. You can have that chair, but you stay off the other one and the couch. Right?"

Lucky thumped his tail in agreement. I gave Buzz an arch look.

"What about me?"

"You can sit anywhere you want." He quickly began moving piles of old comics and clutter off the other easy chair and the couch. "Can you handle more coffee, or would you like beer?"

"Y'know, beer would be great."

The surprising memory of sharp malty bubbles tickled the back of my throat. I hadn't had a beer in decades. It was low class and high fat and I'd taught myself to dislike it when I became a model. Now I declined the offer of a tall glass decorated with a cartoon figure of Goofy and gulped straight from the cold tin of Black Label he handed me from an old round-cornered Maytag fridge barnacled with the largest collection of tacky memo magnets I'd ever seen.

"God, this is good…"

After a long swallow and a discreet burp that drew a smile from Buzz, I tried to remember the last time I'd let go a really satisfying, guiltless loud belch or a thunderous rank fart. Once, I overheard Matthew propounding his theory of the Mystery of Female Flatulence at a party.

"Women don't pass wind. They don't belch and they don't fart because they never eat anything that might cause noxious gasses to accumulate in their bowels. They don't eat beans or chili or anything with too many onions in it." What I remembered most was the odd hostile look he suddenly shot me, which the people he was amusing didn't seem to notice, as if accusing me of trying to pretend my shit didn't stink.

I took a long slow look around the back room. It was messy, but cosy, and there was a faint smell of onions, tomato sauce and accumulated grease in the air.

"Do you live here?"

"Not according to the zoning bylaws, but I've got it rigged up so this room looks just like a workshop. See?"

Lined up along the formica topped workbench there were toasters, kettles, blenders, a waffle-iron, several microwave ovens, a convection-oven, Kitchen Magicians and Veg-O-Matics as seen on TV, even a Cuisinart with a few attachments missing. His kitchen, it occurred to me, was a parody of the one in Laine's condo.

"Plates and cups are out in the shop. Wedgewood, Royal Doulton bone china, stoneware, ironware, Melmac, Bakelite, CorelleWare, anything you want. It may not always match, but I don't often throw dinner parties for six or twelve any-way. More pots and pans than you could shake a shaker at. Electric frypans, T-Fal teflon non-stick, Le Crueset cast-iron, copper bottom Revere ware, whatever. Boxes of cutlery. More utensils than you find could uses for. It's a bit awkward, doing the dishes in the bathroom sink. The bathroom's right there, by the way."

He pointed to an inside door beside the heavily locked and barred back door of the shop. I peered into the tiny room. It was very clean, I noticed, somewhat surprised.

"But how do you take a bath?"

He grinned.

"That was tricky, until I swapped some salvage copper pipe for this."

Like a magician, he lifted the hinged wooden top of what appeared to be a long wooden bench against the back wall, near the door. Inside there was a deep old-fashioned enamelled iron bathtub.

"It's not properly plumbed. I got around that by replacing the old bathroom faucet with one that has threads on the spout. I swapped even on it, though my fixtures were newer, but it was what I needed. Now I just put the plug in the tub and hook up this short garden hose to the tap, turn on the hot and fill the tub. I set the tub on a slight angle with the drain low and welded a catch-pipe to the bottom, also threaded. There's a storm drain right outside the back door. I hook the hose up to the pipe and let gravity do the rest… I mean, I usually have my valet do it, but sometimes I want to take a bath on his night off so…"

I shook my head, amazed.

"It's wonderful. I love these old tubs. They're so deep."

"And long. You can stretch your legs without freezing your shoulders. I even built my own bath-caddy." He took a wooden rack down from a hook on the wall and fitted it across the tub. In the middle, two struts supported an inclined board with a lip to hold a book or magazine in place. On either side, there was a countersunk hole. He dropped a small ashtray into one, his Black Label can into the other. "There you go. And if you plug in this big space heater and drape your towel over it, you've got a hot fluffy terrycloth rubdown when you get out."

Picking up a couple of remote control slabs, he turned on four of the half-dozen television sets, each equipped with VCRs, sharing the opposite wall unit with tape-decks, equalizers, turntables, amps, beat boxes, portable CD players and even an antique eight-track, all linked by a hydra-tangle of wires gathered into makeshift cables with black electricians tape. On one screen, kudus and gazelles bounded effortlessly across the sun-drenched savanna. On another, Godzilla thrashed a bad model of Tokyo to dust with his tail. A luminous Ingrid Bergman pleaded silently for the letters of transit with a suffering stoic Bogart in Casablanca, side by side with a Roadrunner cartoon. He tapped a button and the small room was filled with the sound of Napoleon the Fourteenth singing his banned novelty hit from the Sixties, "They're Coming to Take Me Away, Ha-Ha!"

"If we were uptown, you'd call this multi-media…"

I cracked up, spraying beer down the front of my shirt, thinking of the media-room in Laine's condo, which had cost at least eighty thousand and offered less options. Buzz laughed with me, obviously relieved I hadn't run out of the place screaming.

"I wonder if the dog's hungry?"

Fishing out two big stainless steel mixing-bowls from a box in the main room, he filled one with water and one with a huge helping of the dog food we'd stopped on the way home to buy. He knew a discount pet food shop where he could get good dog chow cheaper by buying in bulk. Lucky jumped off the chair and buried his face in the dish, snorting and crunching.

"That answers that question. What about you? I haven't got anything around here but Kraft Dinner and maybe some Campbell's soup."

I drained my beer.

"It's alright. It's been a long day."

"Yeah." He looked at Lucky who was noisily licking the empty bowl. "We'll take you home."

"Thank you, again… And I meant what I said. I'll pay for his shots and his food and anything else he needs…"

He waved me off.

"Forget it. It's okay. I used to have a cat around the place. He was more dangerous than any dog, especially if anyone bothered him when he'd been drinking."

"Drinking?"

"Yeah. Felix wasn't exactly my cat. I was just his bartender."

"His bartender?"

"We used to live just up and around the corner in an old hotel where I worked the bar for awhile. A shit-pit called The Olympus. Gone now."

"I remember it…"

"You do? You don't look like it was ever your kind of place."

"Well, it wasn't really, but back in high school some of the kids drank there because they never checked ID in the pub. I was underage and terrified I'd get busted so I only went a couple of times. It was actually a sort of hip scene for a little while."

He chuckled.

"Before my time there."

"Yeah. It went back to being a really tough place pretty fast, full of bikers and dope dealers. A girl I knew got killed in the street out front."

He gave me a curiously thoughtful look.

"Shot?"

"How did you know?"

He shrugged.

"Oh, just one of those stories that hang around the places where they happened. People like to tell horror stories, ghost stories, about their own haunts and the O was one of those places that seem to attract people who'd run out of everything but bad luck. I heard it from the regulars in the lounge. That was where I worked. The Blue Parrot cocktail lounge. Was she a friend of yours?"

"Not exactly. She was older, a friend of one of my ex-husband's friends. She helped me get into modelling. She'd actually been a call girl, back before escort services went public, but she quit to do some modelling while she still had her looks, mostly so she could learn to be a photographer. That's why she was down there that night. Taking pictures. She was with Jack Morrison, this friend, when she was killed. He's never really gotten past it. When did they tear it down?"

He gave an odd smile, like he was thinking about something he wasn't going to tell me, but he did tell me something after all.

"They didn't. Oh, the owners wanted to. They let it run down, then tried to have it condemned so they could knock it down and develop the property. That was when Felix and I left. But then some heritage group started making noise, the publisher of the local rag and his cronies. They tied things up with injunctions for a while, so the owners kept the pub open and rented the rooms that still had glass in the windows and working plumbing for a few years. Then some kind of hell broke loose one night and the Mounties called in their swat-team, the ERT, and there was a fire and the whole place came down on a few of them. The arson boys called it a suspicious fire. The cops blamed the owners, the owners blamed the ERT. Felix and I had moved into this place by then. We watched it burn. I managed to salvage this."

He flicked a switch by the curtained door and against the brick back wall of the shop a sign in the shape of a parrot buzzed to life like a mysterious sigil drawn in the air, flooding the room with an eerie pale blue neon glow.

"I remember that! It makes one hell of a nite-lite, though, doesn't it?"

"Yeah."

He snapped off the switch and the blue parrot vanished.

"What happened to Felix?"

"We were roommates and drinking buddies for a few years. I cut off the hard stuff when I took over this place. I limit myself to occasional beers, like a junkie on the chip, but Felix was getting old and set in his ways. He'd lived his whole life in alleys and he couldn't stay out of them. One morning he was a little hungover and slower than a garbage truck, that's all."

"I'm sorry."

He shrugged, but looked away, at the TVs, so I couldn't see his face.

"It was quick. He was getting too old for the backstreet

134

life anyway. Best he could manage was a draw against two or three raccoons. But I miss the little bastard. After him I wouldn't want another cat, but I've thought about getting a dog for a while and this one'll do. I was going to get one from the SPCA and he might've wound up there, if he was lucky."

"He *is* Lucky."

"Yeah, well, Felix had a lot of luck too, but his was mostly bad. Maybe the dog and I will bring each other some good luck. Maybe you, too. It was your good deed."

During the week, I found excuses to drop by the New-To-U. I brought Buzz an Art Deco desk lamp I picked up for nothing from a model who was moving to London. Then I decided to take Lucky for a walk down at Bridgeman Park one slow afternoon when I needed a mental health break away from Laine, hairbrained models, phones and downtown traffic noise. On Friday morning I delivered a surprise picnic lunch for the three of us. Buzz seemed not so much surprised by my visits as a little irritated by the sight of me in full warpaint, silk blouse, leather skirt and high heels. He pretended to be suspicious of the food, holding up a croissant stuffed with smoked salmon and cream cheese and shaking his head dubiously.

"I don't know which of the four food groups this fits into…"

"The four food groups?"

I tried to recall my high school Home Ec. lessons. They'd changed the name to Life Arts or something when I had to take it, but the dull pre-Martha Stewart drill of arcane home-making skills in the textbooks was left over from the Eisenhower years. He ticked them off.

"You know… Kraft Dinner, Campbell soups, sandwiches and burgers…"

"What's the fourth?"

"Beer, of course. I guess you could call this a sandwich. It might be stretching the definition a bit, though."

Still, he ate with good appetite and stuffed croissants washed down with beer broadened my own culinary horizons. Lucky nibbled flakes of pastry from our fingers in the back of the shop. When we were finished, Buzz took a deep breath and invited me to come around for dinner on Sunday if I didn't think I'd be busy, if I didn't have other plans, if I didn't have to wash my hair that night. I accepted as soon as I could get a word in. He was so relieved he told me a story that almost made me regret not playing harder to get.

"I used to do a lot of errands on the bike." He pointed to a dismantled motorcycle out in the main room. "It's cheaper to run than the van. Anyway, one day I got caught in the rain and came in soaked, so I put my wet leather gloves on the shelf over the hot plate to dry and put on a pot of macaroni. I went into the bathroom to get out of the rest of my clothes and start a hot bath and when I came back, one of the gloves had fallen off the shelf into the pot…"

"Oh yuck…"

"Yeah, the macaroni was, well, kind of grey…."

"You didn't?…"

"Of course I did. It was hot. I was cold, wet and hungry and I didn't have anything else to eat. I did have to put some extra cheese and ketchup on it, though. I mean, presentation is everything, right?"

"About Sunday. Anything but…"

"Macaroni."

We had spaghetti instead. He made a good Bolognese, chopping up a couple of sticks of hot pepperoni instead of bland ground beef, sauteeing them with fresh peppers, onions and mushrooms from the Cloverdale market and diced canned tomatoes from a nameless food mart in an alley just off Lonsdale. My appetite was sharpened by a day of dickering in the open air. The sauce had been simmering since the day before and he he'd taken the trouble to nip around to the pasta place on the corner for the fresh stuff, as well as a chunk of Parmesan cheese to grate, fresh Italian bread and ingredients for the Caesar salad tossed in an old plastic salad set I found in the shop. He even picked up a small spray of freesias to go in the CN Hotels bud vase on the card table set up in the front shop. I'd been using it as a kitchen table and brought it to Cloverdale to sell, until Buzz pointed out we could use it for dinner first. I also brought the wine, a reasonable Chianti Classico we sipped from two of the biggest, chunkiest, ugliest, blue glass wine goblets I'd ever seen.

Buzz didn't really drink the wine. He seemed to taste it carefully, even to savour it, but the level in his glass could've dropped faster by evaporation. Over dinner, he explained how he came to own Harry's New-To-U. He'd been a customer, crony and bartender to the last owner, 'Cash' Cohen, whose nickname came from the ancient original sign in the store that said "Debt is the Curse of the Working Class. Our Prices are Low so You can Pay Cash." Cohen actually gave away a lot of things to people who needed them or undercharged to spare their pride. The only people he bargained hard with were trolling antique dealers and slumming interior decorators and he could smell them coming in the door. A post-war Jew who had once been a rabbi, he ran the store casually as a kind of front for his serious secret Zionist activities which sometimes took him behind the Iron Curtain, where he posed as a

Canadian buyer of East German pornography while he worked for the underground railway helping Soviet Jews to escape to Israel.

Cohen bought the shop from Giannakis, an amiable Greek who wanted it only so he and his pals would have a sort of private club where they could sip ouzo and play backgammon all day without being nagged by their wives. He'd bought it from the widow of the original Harry, a phantom English reprobate remittance man who went back home to join the British Army in 1914 to defend King, Country and Empire and was promptly turned into sausage meat by the Germans in Flanders. Some of the original stock still remained in the shop, buried under layers of artifacts it would take a team of archaeologists to find and classify.

"Someone should write a history of the people who've owned this shop."

Buzz laughed softly.

"You know *The Maltese Falcon?* Bogart and Mary Astor? Sidney Greenstreet and Peter Lorre? Greenstreet plays Gutman, the Fat Man, and the crucial scene is when he tells Sam Spade the history of the Black Bird, how it's stolen from the Knights of St. John by pirates and turns up in a Paris antique store run by a Greek but the store mysteriously burns and the bird surfaces in Istanbul in the house of a Russian general. That's the scene that hooks you. There's no action in it at all, just talk, but that's the scene that gives this dumb object, this weird curio, a kind of sacred power by reciting its history, a litany of human greed and coveting, even to the point of murder. That's what really makes the falcon so valuable. Bogart's line when he has them all together in his apartment, 'I know what value in human life you people put on it'…is the whole movie."

The candles burned down in two actually matching candlesticks, twin Italian fantasies in rococco wrought iron. In the flickering light, the shop became a fairy tale Cave of The Forty Thieves, filled with wonderful and mysterious treasure. Even Lucky, noisily slurping leftovers from his dish under the table, couldn't break the spell. When we finished, Buzz suggested with mock formality we retire to the drawing room to finish our wine. Coffee burbled on the hot plate in an old percolator with glass bulb in the top while we watched the original *Invasion of The Body Snatchers* on the largest of the TVs. Buzz had stacks of videos of old science fiction and horror movies.

"I like them because they have happy endings in spite of the monsters."

I told him about Matthew then, thinking he might be interested, about his novels and his collaborations with Frank Steinberg, but immediately wished I hadn't. Watching him grope for something polite to say made me feel like a pretentious name-dropper who'd just been trying to impress him.

"His early books weren't bad. I hung onto a first edition of *Waspworks* for a while, until a fan offered me a really good price for it. Canadian first editions have smaller press runs than American ones, so they're rarer and increase their value faster, especially if an American edition comes out. I'm not a big fan of Steinberg, though. His films are cold. There's no innocence, I guess you'd call it. That's what I like about these old flicks. They're fairy tales. The good guys win. The evil mutants or aliens lose. The hero always saves the Mad Scientist's daughter when she trips and twists her ankle when she's running away from the monsters. But like real fairy tales, they're not as simple as they seem. Like the way the hero is often a young scientist while the villain is a Mad Scientist and his daughter is the muse they fight over. The single monster, like Dr. Frankenstein's reanimated patchwork corpse, or Count Dracula, or Godzilla, or the single alien like Michael Rennie in *The Day The Earth Stood Still,* are actually characters you sympathize with up to a point, because their existence brings out the worst in normal people, the reflex hatred of anything or anyone different. But when you multiply the monsters or aliens, they're always portrayed as brutal fascists with an insect hive mentality…"

When he put on the second feature, I realized I was going to have to take the bull by something other than the horns if I wanted more than popcorn. I did it by going out to the front shop to clear up the dishes. Buzz followed me.

"You don't have to…"

I turned and wrapped my arms around his neck in a near choke-hold. Then I kissed him hard enough to make myself understood by a marble statue. He had the decency not to struggle. The couch in the back pulled out into a double bed. I'd been wondering where he slept, but I should've figured. I didn't even mind that we made love end for end, with our feet on the pillows, so we could watch *War of The Worlds* while we were doing it. It made me feel like a teenager again, the long slow slippery grinding against each other in the cathode glow, the muted screams and explosions on the Friday Night Horror TV double features lulling the dozing parents upstairs into the certainty that nothing more serious than the destruction of the world could be happening below.

But now there was nothing furtive, no hurried hiking up of jeans, wet underwear twisted in the crack of your butt, no creaking door or footstep on the stairs, no parental voice blandly offering hot chocolate or a Coke at intervals when it was judged to have been too quiet for too long. An orgasm struck as violently and unexpectedly as the Martian attack on the world's major cities and my short sharp affirmative cry was drowned out by the electronic stacatto of alien death-rays. We hung together in a kind of entropic free-fall until the swelling music of the credits signalled the world had been saved once more.

Afterwards, I nestled against him when he came back from sliding yet another cassette, *The Time Machine*, into the VCR. My eyes were glazing over and I let them close, content to lie there, drifting in and out of sleep, listening to snatches of the movie and secretly sympathizing with the Morlocks, ugly cannibal creatures doomed to be slaves of the underground industrial machinery of night while the beautiful Eloi frolicked uselessly in the sun. Unnoticed by Buzz, who lay on his stomach watching the screen with his chin propped up by a can of Black Label, Lucky climbed up on the bed and curled up against the hollow of my back. Between them, I fell asleep, safe from the future.

Chapter 12

From the moment I got to The Agency Monday morning I felt like I was trapped in a waterslide park at a sewage treatment plant. One of my clients, only a year or two younger though she acted like we were from different generations, was in crisis because her career wasn't moving to the next level. Too petite for the runway, she'd modelled more in magazine ads and done a few commercials for local TV stations the sponsors liked enough to take national. People would recognize her at Stamps Landing or Bridges as "*That girl…the one who does the whatever ad…on TV…*"

That Girl as played by the young Marlo Thomas, who predated the obviously middle-aged Mary Tyler Moore as our role model on after-school re-runs, she wasn't. Her best feature was her mouth, superabundant lips untouched by the collagen needle, to which major cosmetic firms still paid lucrative homage. For someone who needed both her bra and the backside of her panties inflated by the special effects department to break into the third dimension, I thought she'd done pretty well out of one body part. Lip models are a cut above the girls we call The Digits, foot and finger models who specialize in shoes, rings, hand creams and nail polish.

I found out why when I accompanied her on a TV commercial shoot and overheard the director talking to Chris, there to shoot still frames, refer to her as 'Hoover.' They both snickered knowingly, making soft slurping sounds. Sucking or fucking your way into jobs gives models a bad name and makes agents look like pimps, so it's officially frowned on. I hadn't said anything to Laine yet. Whether she already knew or not, and I assumed she did, saying it openly about one of our steady high-earners would make me as popular as a waitress with a large running cold sore.

But knowing made it hard to listen to Hoover's bitching. In her mind, Vanna White was a serious actress who'd paid her dues on a popular game show for twenty years and ought to be getting the kind of major film roles she herself expected to be offered as soon as certain people in the industry woke up and smelled the money. She thought Vanna could have played Ophelia to Mel Gibson's Hamlet better than Helena Bonham Carter. I didn't tell her I thought Mel's Hamlet belonged on the menu at Denny's or that Vanna would have had a better shot going up against Glenn Close in the casting call for Hamlet's mom. The implication that I, as the operator in charge of delivering the wake-up call, was napping on the job wasn't lost on me. While her adenoidal whine filled up my office, I envied Lisa her life sentence in the protective custody of silence.

I didn't blame Chris, though I wished he'd bothered to

look over his shoulder before getting into the Boys Room banter. When he was in high school with Matthew, Chris had seen Antonioni's film, *Blow-Up*. The sequence where the young fashion photographer writhes on a pull-down screen of purple paper with two nymphette wanna-be models convinced him this was the life for him. To his own surprise he discovered he had the instinctive eye and inventive darkroom skills to make a living at it. When I introduced him to Laine he was driving a night-shift cab with a police radio scanner, three cameras, a glovebox full of film and a trunk filled with empty pizza boxes, chasing ambulances and cop cars instead of fares, selling freelance news pics to the daily papers and tabloids and shooting rolls of gritty social realism and Diane Arbus-style freaks on the downtown eastside.

With a wave of her hundred-mil nicotine wand, Laine made his youthful fantasy come true and he found himself making a lot more money taking pictures of people who didn't have knife scars, needles hanging out of their arms and hadn't pissed their pants recently. He had, he admitted to me once, even tried to duplicate the purple paper scene.

"The girls were up for it after a few rails of coke, but they really didn't get it. Too young. Never saw the film… And all that purple paper really got in the way. It was dry and gave me a rash."

His disappointment was so genuinely naive, so like a boy who sends away the coupon from the comic for a Hundred Civil War Soldiers only to get a teeny bag of minuscule two-dimensional figures stamped out of cheap plastic after six weeks of ambushing the mailman, it was impossible not to love him for it. Though Chris no longer believed David Bowie was the Second Coming of the Electronic Christ, he still looked like Bowie in his post-Ziggy Stardust Thin White Duke incarnation, somehow boyish under the blonde-streaks that hid the creeping gray.

By the time I finally got Hoover out of my office everyone else had gone for the day but Chris. I bumped into him at the staff room fridge while looking for a blueberry yogurt or something to recharge my battery for the drive back to the postmodern oxymoron of my increasingly minimalist apartment. Anjou pear and Evian water in hand, he looked whipped and I told him so. He nodded sadly.

"It's the strain of trying to make all these empty beautiful faces look human. I'm developing my own conspiracy theory that beautiful people are proof aliens are among us doing an X-files number. Not invading directly, but subtly interbreeding and genetically engineering a hybrid species that will inherit the earth by default. They're like the people in that old movie, *The Time Machine*…"

"The Eloi."

"Yeah. That's it. Yvette what'shername…"

"Mimieux."

"And that Aussie guy…"

"Rod Taylor."

"Yeah. Hey, you're really up on this old shit."

I smiled to myself.

"Saw it on the Late Show the other night."

"Yeah. Well, I remember when I read the book. H.G. Wells. Man, him and Jules Verne, Orwell and Huxley. I always liked Wells best. *The Mysterious Island of Doctor Moreau*…"

"Wasn't Bela Lugosi in the old black and white?…"

"Yeah. There's been a lot of remakes, with Burt Lancaster and Marlon Brando playing the Doctor and better makeup, but the original captures the mood of the book best. I used to read those books, you know? I don't even know where they are now. The other night I looked through my bookshelf for something to read and all I could find were stacks of magazines and old copies of *TV Week*. The only books there were by writers whose photos I'd done for the book jackets. Matthew's of course…"

He shot me a nervous look as he dared to say Matthew's name, since we'd both carefully avoided the subject of the divorce for fear of jeopardizing both our friendship and working relationship.

"They're still good pictures, Chris."

He shrugged dismissively as we drifted down the iron spiral staircase to the deserted studio.

"They're shit, Eve. The Writer, sitting at his Desk, in front of the Great Wall of Books. Trite crap. I mean, I should have shot him puking in the street or squatting on the bowl, dropping a big steamer. The Great Writer Serving It Up to His Public."

"I thought you were a fan…and Matthew's friend."

"He's called me exactly once since you two split and then he only wanted to get the buzz on what you were doing. But hey, I'm a fan of anybody who gets away with doing what they love and makes a living at it. The problem is, your work becomes what others see in it and you make out by pretending to be someone else, just like the guy who humps trashcans. Jack worked the garbage trucks with guys who have degrees in philosophy, some who play chess at grandmaster level. But they don't make a living at it, so to the world they're just one guy leaning on a shovel and four guys supervising him. No picture I could take would change the way people see them, just like you could bring an eighteen-year-old girl in here with a degree in atomic physics, who just happened to be tall, blonde and beautiful. What would we turn her into? A model! All people would see is a skinny girl with too much makeup who looks good in clothes or lingerie, but sprawled out naked on a bed looks like something dumped in a lime pit at a death camp in an old newsreel…"

I licked the last of my yogurt off the white plastic spoon while Chris watched with an interest that made my scalp tingle, like an unexpected breeze loosening my hair from its invisible net of mousse. Pinching a pack of Pall Mall cigarettes out of his shirt pocket, he shot one halfway out of the crumpled red pack with a graceful twist of his wrist, offering me a hundred millimetres of unfiltered tobacco. He seemed suddenly fascinated with my mouth, so I took it with my lips instead of my fingers and dipped the end in the wavering blue flame of the stainless steel Zippo he pulled from the pocket of this tight black jeans, flicked open and alight in one slick juvenile delinquent motion.

"Don't tell me you're losing interest in your work? I thought women were your favourite subjects…"

I tried to keep the tone light and bantering, but he grimaced and snapped the Zippo shut with a gesture of disgust at the walls plastered with head and body shots of models.

"These aren't women. I lost interest in models after the first six months. Even when they're screwing they seem to be posing for some invisible lens. You know, I was actually in bed with one of these girls one night, going at it hammer and nails, fang and claw, her heels up around my ears, and right in the middle of this ecstatic experience she says, 'I don't like this position. It makes my ass look fat.'…My first thought was,

'How the fuck does she know whether or not her ass looks fat?' Then I realized she was looking past my shoulder at the mirrored doors of the closet, watching herself fuck and worrying about how she looked doing it. It would've been kinder to just turn a cold hose on me, like they do to dogs copulating in the street up north…"

I laughed through a deliciously nostalgic cloud of pungent American blended tobaccos. Chris chuckled bitterly. He was in serious mode here.

"That's what I loved about Amanda. She was so vivid, so sensitive, so intelligent, so real, compared to the vague vapid twats I was shooting…"

"And scoring…"

I kept laughing, forcing it a bit, because I really didn't want to hear another replay of the post-mortem on his relationship with Amanda, especially when I suspected she'd only married him for his DNA. Through both her pregnancies she smugly talked about how she and Chris were bequeathing their children 'good genes,' like some Nazi eugenicist or show-dog breeder, implying that less scrupulous couples who procreated weren't families so much as unlicensed human puppy-mills. That their toddlers actually did both look like *putti* descended from a Michaelangelo fresco only made it worse. Though I wouldn't have wished a flawed child on anyone, I knew in some small dark secret place in my heart I'd hoped they might have a least one they'd have to name Caliban or Medusa.

"I know it's funny, talking about it now, like this, but it isn't funny at three in the morning when you're thinking about your life… Your marriage is over, your kids aren't there and you can't even find any of your favourite old books."

I stopped laughing.

"No. You're right, Chris. It isn't funny. And now Amanda's being vivid and real and sensitive and intelligent with your friend Michael, whose feelings for me were so real and sensitive and deep he couldn't be bothered to actually break up with me. How low do you want to go here? Because I think the pit I'm in is deeper than yours. At least Amanda had the decency to marry you and legally dump you. I haven't even officially been dumped. I'm still waiting for the Dear Jane letter with no return address, the don't call back message on the answering machine, the ice cream cake delivered with 'It's Over, You Stupid Cunt' in black marzipan icing…"

I started to sniffle in spite of myself, not because I was sad, but because I suddenly wanted to kick Michael in the nuts, very hard, and his nuts weren't in range. Chris put his long arms around me, filling my nose with Givenchy cologne.

"I'm sorry, Eve. I shouldn't have…" He cupped my chin in his fingers and lifted it so he could see my face. "My God, you're such a lovely woman. Not a girl. Not a model. A woman. I'd really like to photograph you… Now… Not as you are, vulnerable and wounded, but with your makeup fixed. Triumphant pictures that celebrate you, that capture the beauty and power of your mature womanly sensuality. Pictures that make these teenage bimbos with their precocious faux sexiness look like the sleazy porn reels in the old quarter machines at Coin City. Pictures that show a woman who's had those superficial good looks, but who's evolved and become suffused with a feminine wisdom passed on from time immemorial and become truly beautiful, a goddess, the original Eve…"

I was suddenly aware his hands had dropped to my waist,

where his fingertips were ever-so-lightly drawing little circles on the tops of my hip bones. My head felt like it usually did after three glasses of cheap Spanish *cava*. No one had really wanted to take my picture in five, honestly maybe ten years. And no one in almost twenty years had wanted to take a picture of me as me, for its own sake, without considering whether or not my face or body could sell cars, tampons, high fashion rags or Borax. Chris ushered me into the dressing room off the main studio.

"Slip into something filmy, something you're comfortable with. We'll shoot a roll or two to relax. Then, if you're as honest and brave as I think you are, we'll shoot some tasteful nudes. Nothing tacky. Soft lighting, soft focus. Bit of Vaseline on the lens. I want to capture a mood of timeless sensuality which extends the frame of the photograph itself and turns it into an icon…"

Unbuttoning my silk blouse in the small cool room crowded with filing cabinets, everything draped with prop clothes like a thrift store in an upscale neighbourhood, I felt my nipples tingling slightly. What the fuck was I doing? In all the years I'd known and worked with Chris, even before we moved to Toronto, he'd never made even the most tentative sexual pass at me. Okay, I was his friend's girl or wife then. Now I was absolutely certain this photo session was going to end in a wrestling match and some nasty stains on the purple paper. Metaphorically, since I doubted he'd be tacky enough to actually use purple, knowing I had seen the movie.

But since I never had wanted to fuck Chris and still didn't, why was I standing here in a draft with nipples hard as pencil erasers and a case of rising damp in my sensible workday Warner briefs? Was it the coincidental talk about Wells,

The Time Machine, the memory of the surprise *War of The Worlds* orgasm with Buzz last weekend, resonating and reverberating in all those millions of nerve ends God mischievously pinched together in the most inconvenient high-traffic area of the female body?

Dropping my skirt and peeling off my Warners I turned and studied myself in the full length mirror on the back of the door. This was what it was about, the slight droop in the gravity-defying tits, shrunk by dieting instead of suckling, the belly still a flat testament to self-denial, a wilderness untracked by stretch-marks, just beginning to slacken with laziness and time. Eyes swollen from crying, surrounded by faint prophetic tracks where crows would land to peck them out. Lips that once promised bliss, turning down at the corners, thinning and tightening with disappointment. All pathetic under hair so expertly disarranged and highlighted it looked like a wig. The face that launched a thousand shipments of cosmetics, now just a cartoon mask of desperate narcissistic lust.

Buzz hadn't paused to admire the gift I was giving him with the customary awe and wonder. I'd have been disappointed in him if he had, yet I was secretly unnerved because he hadn't. I was ashamed of wanting more than to be simply and honestly desired, yet I wanted someone to make all this beautiful again. I wanted it so badly I was prepared to do anything Chris asked me to do if he could only transform what I saw in the mirror in the harsh light of that small room into beauty.

I took a deep breath and leaned against one of the fireproof file cabinets storing his negatives and prints. There was a fresh file folder under my nails, which needed a manicure, I noticed. I flicked the folder open.

Lisa stared up at me, apparently wearing nothing but an oversize man's white shirt, the collar turned up like Juliette Greco in the 50's, big French cuffs folded loosely back up her thin forearms. One of Chris' favourite props, it covered her like a dress, but the buttons were undone to the navel and she sprawled languidly among heavy white linen blackout curtains rucked up to suggest the well-tumbled sheets of an enormous bed. Her makeup was very good, not enough to disguise her innocence, just enough to be used by the photographer as defence against a charge of disseminating child pornography or statutory rape.

Sour slimy blueberry yogurt crawled up my throat into my mouth. I thumbed quickly through the stack of prints. No hardcore. Not here anyway.

There was a discreet tap on the door.

"I'm just about set up out here. Are you ready?"

"Uh… Almost. Half a minute."

Sweeping the prints into my purse, I got dressed faster than if the fire alarm was clanging. Frantically I scanned the room, looking for an equalizer. Jack Morrison and Harry Lamb had given me a few lessons in practical self-defence over the years. When he drove cab, Jack kept an old glass Coke bottle filled with sand, sealed with wax and wrapped with adhesive tape, under the seat. A big heavy Craftsman wrench or ratchet arm is an innocent tool every woman ought to have in the side pocket of the driver's door, because one good stroke can crack a skull or shatter a human forearm, he told me. Jack also suggested I carry a few rolls of nickels or quarters at the bottom of my purse.

"Swing a bag with a couple of rolls of coin against the side of some dude's head, it's like hitting him with a lead pipe.

Clench a roll in your fist, you double the power of your punch. It's called 'making change,' as in 'I had a guy in my cab last night who gave me a big bill, meaning big trouble, so I had to make change.'"

Harry Lamb played bass in Vancouver's legendary punk band, Metal Fatigue, before he became a Lord. His reputation for violence was based on his skill at whipping a Fender Precision over his shoulder and down on the heads of front row fans foolish enough to voice their disapproval of Metal Fatigue's musical evolution. Harry's tenure as Laine's young man had been the shortest on record. When she used her pull to get him an interview with some A&R types from a major American label, he burst into their suite at the Four Seasons wearing kneepads, swept a thousand dollars worth of cocaine off the coffee table into the shag Berber with a flail of his arm and replaced it with a jar of Vaseline.

"Boys, I'll do the necessary for a contract. Who wants to be first?" When Laine found out he also bragged in public about refusing to fuck her west of Main Street, insisting on shagging her across the leather seats of the Porsche in danger-ous parking lots behind the Smiling Buddha, he went back to being a legend forever. Raised in the north of England until he was fourteen, Harry taught me the Liverpool Kiss. You simply grab your assailant by the ears, snap his head forward and slam your forehead into the bridge of his nose as hard as you can. I wished he or Jack were with me now to deal with their old pal Chris.

Among the clutter on top of the filing cabinets I found a film bag and lenses. Picking out the biggest, heaviest, most blatantly penile lens, I dropped it into the bag and opened the door. Chris was standing outside, adjusting the F-stop of his motor-driven Nikon.

"Eve? You haven't changed…"

"Oh but I have."

I swung the bag overhand. It struck somewhere near the bridge of his nose and he dropped, covering his face and collapsing to the floor with an anguished squeak. When he started to get up, blood welling through fingers splayed across his face, I clipped him across the temple with a backhand I wouldn't have been ashamed to show Laine at the Vancouver Lawn Tennis Club. Chris dropped to the floor with a groan like a pole-axed stoat. Halfway up the spiral staircase, I tossed the bag over my shoulder and heard it hit the refinished, distressed wood floor with the satisfying crunch of expensive precision-ground lens turning into garbage.

Chapter 13

An interested quiet prevailed at The Agency next morning. Nothing was said, but everyone seemed to be waiting for something unspecified to happen. Chris had to come in because he was on deadline on a job. From my expectantly ajar office door, I saw him cross the foyer quickly, the bridge of his nose encased in fresh white medical tape and a large blue egg spoiling the hairline on the right side of his head. He didn't look my way.

Laine glanced curiously in my direction on the way to her office, from which she emerged after half an hour on the phone to announce loudly to Gail the receptionist she had a meeting and wouldn't be back until late afternoon. She left without a word to me and I assumed Chris had called her the night before, probably from the hospital for dramatic effect, and filled in his half of the accident report. Aware of his flair for retouching prints, dodging negatives, even staging supposed news photographs in the old days, at least she was too smart to believe the camera never lies. On the other hand, if he'd missed the prints of Lisa already, he might've told her he'd walked into a door or got in a fight at a nightclub.

Not long after Laine left, Lisa showed up. Why wasn't she in school? She went straight down the spiral staircase to the studio like she had an appointment. I was out of my chair and almost to the door of my office when she came back up as if her shoes were on fire. Instead of heading out the office doors, she dashed straight into my office and sat down, grabbing a notepad from the desk and scribbling.

did you really do that to him?

I shrugged and nodded. She gave me a fierce look that seemed a bit calculated to me.

why????

I sat down, took the prints out of my bag and fanned them on the desk. Her face became a circus parade of emotions; sulkiness, defiance, embarrassment, fear, pride and mischievousness. I wrote on another pad and spun it toward her.

popcorn?

She gave me a confused look, then printed her answer neatly.

no thank you you did that because of me?

I took my pad back and wrote another question.

you told me you hated modelling. you thought it was phoney. so why did you pose for these pictures?

She shrugged, turning sullen and teenage for a moment. Then she looked at me thoughtfully and wrote her answer with care.

I wanted to see myself differently. thats all. like an actor.

I wrote back with equal restraint.

but you already do that. In your writing. I think your story is wonderful. I read it over every night.

She couldn't suppress a blush of pride, though her answer tried to play it down.

but when I write its just me imagining myself as someone different in a world I imagined its all in my head just words on paper I wanted to SEE a picture of myself that looked different I think the pictures are really cool but they're like a story that isn't really ME.

I sighed.

That's what every actress tells herself when she decides to take a terrible role in a shitty movie. Or when a model decides to do a porn shoot.

That stung. She pouted. Obviously I didn't get it. She was using this experience as a form of play, like dressing up in old clothes and costumes, exploring and expressing her possible identities while I was being narrow minded and judgmental. Not to forget old. I wasn't going to win this round on points. I tapped my pen on the pad for a while before I wrote again.

the difference is that when you write a story you control how the reader sees everything and even how they feel its your imagination your insight your power completely. when you pose for pictures like these or even model for catalogues you don't have the power. The photographer does. some art director does. your agent does. you're just an object like a prop on a set in a play that someone else uses to create a story or an impression usually to sell something.

She read this over a couple of times. When she looked at the photographs again she didn't look as pleased with herself.

are you going to show these to Mom?

I chewed the end of my pen for awhile before answering.
probably.

Crestfallen and hostile, she sagged in her chair, scrawling.

she won't care she'll be proud she'll think they're CUTE she'll probably have them blown up and framed and hang them in her fucking ugly living room

I shook my head as I wrote back.

you're missing the point. its not about YOU expressing yourself or seeing yourself differently or any of that shit. I have to show them to your mother because a photographer who works for a professional agency your mother happens to own took these kind of shots of a 14 year old girl. I'd have to do this if it was ANY 14 year old girl. mothers bring their daughters here to be trained as models and actors. they know the business. they know the risks. in spite of them they trust us to not to exploit their children.

Lisa slammed her pad on the desk, grinding her nib into the paper.

but THEYRE exploiting their children! For $$$$$$!!!

I took a deep breath and wrote back.

Yes. thats what this industry does. it uses beauty and talent to sell things and it pays very well. some parents do push their children into it when the kids aren't interested. but they DONT bring their kids here to have us get them addicted to cocaine or have them sleep with 40 yr old photographers who take hardcore pictures of them and sell them to magazines or over the Internet. if they get just the slightest whiff that might be what happens here your mother will be ruined. bankrupt. BROKE. if certain parents saw pictures like these of their daughter YOUR mother could be sued—maybe arrested and put in jail. no more condo in Kits. no more special tutors for you. no more trips to Hawaii or

London or Paris. no more money for your Grandma. your Grandma could wind up boxing Tim-Bits for truck drivers on the midnight shift while YOU mop floors at the 7-11. do you understand how serious this is?

She didn't, but she was trying. I added one final note.

Chris is exploiting his friendship with your mother. he's abusing it, abusing her and abusing you and putting your whole lives at risk. I only hope hes not abusing you in the way these pictures suggest.

I hated myself for writing something like a social worker fishing for hints to make a case. Lisa looked shocked enough at the suggestion I was hugely relieved. Even if he'd started with the sly hand 'arranging' the shirt from underneath, gently stroking here and there, he hadn't done anything more. My little office seemed hotter than a steam room. Lisa was scrawling on my notepad.

he didn't! I didn't! nothing happened! it was just

I snatched the pad away and threw it in the trash, sliding the photos into my bag, trusting her to read my lips.

"Lets go. Lets go out for coffee... No something cold. Iced lattes. Gelati. Ice cream."

Lisa reached across and wrote on my pad.

Big Gulp Slurpee?

We bought a dragon kite at Go Fly A Kite on Water St., and two huge soft drinks full of shaved ice in takeout cartons the size of buckets from the Fifties retro diner up the block. Driving east along Powell St. the Mini bouncing over railroad tracks past the old Rogers Sugar refinery, I cut along Wall St. and checked out the light chop on the Inlet. A brisk breeze was fluffing the billows. At New Brighton Park, we unrolled the long simple kite. Lithe and quick as a deer dashing across the grass, Lisa had it up in moments, a brilliant banner against the cool blue sky.

Taking turns flying the kite, we lazed and sucked our slurpees and didn't write any notes. She didn't have to read my lips because I didn't say anything. We were just two girls cutting classes to fly a kite. I lay on the grass watching Lisa smile up at the kite undulating in the wind and had one of those weird moments of *deja vu*. Not that I felt like I'd been there before exactly, but I remembered years ago Jack Morrison quoted an old Chinese poem to me when I was having an anxiety attack about moving to Toronto. How did it go?… Darkness rises on the road behind… Up ahead in the hills, a tiger roars… At such times the traveller's heart is a banner…a hundred feet high in the wind… Something like that. Seeing Lisa with the kite must've made me think of it.

For the first time in years, my heart really did feel like a kite, a flag a hundred feet high in the wind. Unfortunately just at the moment, there was a stitch of envy under it. For an hour in the sun I could play pretend, imagine Lisa was the daughter I didn't have, but it only made me angry at Laine, whose idea of quality time with her daughter was trying on clothes too young for her, too old for Lisa and too expensive for anyone having an episode of sanity at Holt Renfrew in some upscale mall. Despite Laine's streetwise manner, it would never occur to her to spend ten bucks on a cheap kite and drink a quart of simple syrup and soda from a cardboard tub in a public park.

I drove Lisa to back to school where she belonged and battled the bumper car traffic downtown, my heart still aloft on the wind. At The Agency, the foyer looked like the main downtown bus terminal. Gail's switchboard was lit up like a tote board, the phones were twittering like a flock of condor chicks and Gail was rinsing a Prozac down with a bottle of flat Perrier. She pointed to my desk, covered with pink message memos. I winked at her and spread my arms, rising up on my toes.

"Ah, the cherry blossoms are falling…"

She gave me a rolled-back eyes 'Oh shit, you've gone nuts too' look and retreated to her desk. I called to her over my shoulder as I strode into my office.

"Send in whoever's been waiting longest and send in the next victim after exactly ten minutes." I said it loud enough for the two dozen people posing on the leather couches and leaning on the art walls to hear. "They've got ten to make their pitch or bitch their bitch, then it's someone else's kick at my can."

For the next four hours I schmoozed, smoothed, stroked and smoked with the window open and the door closed, told aspiring actors to stick with modelling or go into sales, advised aspiring models to get some kind of trade skills, dump the drug dealer boyfriend or just cut to the chase and hire out to an escort service while their looks were still worth something, all the while returning phone calls with decisive replies and making tiny pink airplanes with the memos, most of which did not fly as well as the kite, nose-diving to the floor around my desk.

In the middle of one emergency call from a catalogue photographer while a hunky young actor flexed his deltoids and steroids impatiently in the opposite chair, I realized I was too damn hot, so I took off my pantyhose. Shocked and fascinated, he watched me kick off my shoes, decorously hike my skirt and squirm out of the nylon sausage casing in my chair while carrying on with the call. Screened by the desk, it was all perfectly decent, but by the time I hung up and dropped the handful of black gauze into the wastebasket, he'd completely forgotten what he came in for.

"Sorry about that. You were saying?"

He stood up to leave, then hesitated, glancing at the wastebasket.

"Uh…Can I…Can I *have* them?"

Picking the crushed ball of nylon out of the trash, I tossed it over my shoulder out the open window onto Water Street.

"No dibbsies. If you can find 'em, they're yours to drag across your face."

He was gone like the Roadrunner in the cartoons. Around five-thirty a courier delivered a plain envelope addressed to me. I told my last interview she needed a therapist, not an agent, passed her the card of a local psychiatrist, Dr. Stern's parting gift to me, never used, and fingernailed the flap. Inside were half a dozen sheets of printed text with a hand-written title in decorative ink.

Chapter 14

On the way back to the apartment, I stopped at the Harbour Centre liquor store and picked up a six-pack of Black Label tins, avoiding the brandy shelves. Trapped in traffic, I reached into the back seat, yanked one loose and popped it in my lap, clutching it between my bare thighs, savouring the cool smooth round shape, lifting it to my lips and sucking foam with delinquent glee. Who'd suspect the cranberry cooler or glass-of-chardonnay career girl of guzzling warm beer from a lap-can? As I rounded the corner into the immaculate alley behind Hemlock Street, I tossed the empty out the window of the Mini, hearing it bounce rudely into the bindweed-choked hedge. It was still broad daylight, but the lifestyle police didn't pull me over, strip-search me for tattoos or put me in a re-education camp.

The Mini parked, I hooked the remaining beers and my slingbacks over my shoulder and took long bold strides down the hall, hearing deadbolts slam into jamb-slots behind me as neighbours backed away from their spy-holes in terror at the sight of a barefoot woman armed with domestic beer. Locking the door, I stripped to the skin in the hall, kicking skirt, blouse, bra and panties into a corner. I fished a funky long t-shirt out of the laundry basket, pulled another tin out of the loop, popped it and sucked off the foam, shoved the rest in the fridge to chill and sat at the the kitchen table by the window with my beer and Lisa's story.

Unfolding the pages, I read the title: *The Friends.*

The long line of men chained together at the neck wove like a snake through troughs between waves of sand. Pools of darkness rose like a tide to engulf all but the moonlit tops of the dunes. At last the snake slowed and coiled upon itself. After receiving a mouthful of water from a robed figure who moved among them, the men collapsed into exhausted sleep on the cooling sand. They were of all shapes, sizes and colours—black men from the jungles of the south, brown men from the deserts of the east, even a few white men from the northern forests beyond the great sea.

One of these only pretended to sleep. This night his struggle with the slave collar was rewarded. His chains dropped silently into the soft sand. The guards had drawn their robes about them and huddled together like piles of filthy linen against the cold desert night. Whispering a charm to preserve their sleep, the man eased from his place and crept away with the smooth unhurried purpose of a snake. Keeping to the darkest patches of shadow, at last he reached a place where darkness shrouded all but the very tip of a dune. Mouthing a prayer, he scuttled up the treacherous slope, his eyes fixed on the small pool of bright moonlight at the top. For an instant, he would be visible there, a flitting shadow. Then he would be free.

Exultantly he crept into the light, risking a glance over his shoulder. The camp was quiet. The robed sleepers had not seen him. Then, as he turned to drop into the inky shadows on the far side of the dune, darkness reached out and struck him with a huge black fist. Stunned, he sprawled on his back in the pool of light. The stars flashed across the sky into his eyes and an enormous shadow slipped over him, swinging the crescent moon like a scythe. But the moon was full, a great blind white eye staring down at him from the star-sprinkled sky.

The tip of a long curved sword hovered just above his nose, its hilt held lightly by a giant, hidden by robes blacker than the shadows. White eyes and teeth glowed with malevolent amusement out of his black face. The white man knew him now. The leader of the slavers, who the others called The Silent One as they hurried to obey his wordless commands. There were shouts from the camp, but the black giant silenced them by raising the sword over his head. The sword began to descend.

"Wait!" the white man cried, "Before you strike, hear me!"

Again the tip of the sword danced before his eyes, weaving hypnotically like a cobra about to lash out. The black figure towered over him like an obsidian idol. He felt he was in the presence of some terrible, implacable god.

"I am a King!" he cried, "A son of kings! When I was a boy, my father fought the Romans. He was defeated but became their ally. I was sent to Rome to study until the day I would be King. After many years, news came my father had died. I sailed on a ship to return to my people and claim my throne, but the ship was taken by pirates and I was sold as a slave. If you will escort me to my homeland, I promise your reward shall be the ransom of a King!"

The black giant remained silent and motionless. The white

man continued more confidently.

"Think of it!... Riches! Luxury! Slaves of your own! Never again to cross these pitiless sands! I alone am worth more to you than all those wretches! Slay them here and leave them for the eaters of the dead! When you and your men have brought me to the sea, we can take ship and..."

The black giant threw back his head and his laughter filled the desert night like the mocking cry of a hyena. It was the first sound the white man had ever heard him make.

"A King!" he said, his voice now the low growl of a lion, "A son of Kings! Well, your majesty, I will tell you what I know of Kings and men..." His eyes narrowed to slits and his voice became soft as he gestured with his free hand to encompass the desert which stretched like a motionless sea in every direction.

"Once all this was only part of a kingdom greater even than the conquests of the Romans. From the Land of the Black Men, from the Mountains of the Gods, the source of the River of Life, to the lands beyond the Great Sea, all this was ruled by one man alone... King Juba...

"A man of the desert, King Juba was born to war. His mother was a woman of the Sea People who once crossed mountains and seas with their war elephants to attack Rome itself. But King Juba had always been a friend to Rome and the Romans so esteemed his friendship they sent him an ambassador as a hostage. Son of an ancient, noble family, this man Petrius was schooled in the arts of war and government. Though he loved to compose odes and play his lyre, he often crossed swords with King Juba in training. They tested each other's skill with all manner of weapons and Petrius taught the King how the Romans make war and govern those they conquer.

"King Juba loved Petrius well. Together they rode and hunt-

ed, often sharing their last drop of water and last mouthful of bread in the desert. When they caroused, if the King grew melancholy with wine, only a song from Petrius could cheer him...

"But in time messengers brought evil news from Rome. One of her greatest generals from the North had rebelled and led his legions against Rome itself. He meant to make himself King of Rome. King Juba did not understand the Roman horror of kings and he thought it perverse of them to appoint a general to put down the rebel who was related to him by marriage, but their distant quarrels did not concern him...

"Yet Petrius pressed King Juba to prepare for war. Though he was happy in the kingdom of his friend and had almost forgotten he was a Roman, his ancestors had sat in the ruling council of the city for generations. He brooded, forgetting his lyre, and exchanged his cool robes for the stiff leather tunic and armour of a Roman soldier. Drilling himself to exhaustion, he once nearly killed the King in sword practice.

"When the usurper's army marched into the country of King Juba, Petrius advised the King to retreat, letting heat and thirst weaken their foes. Then, when the whole Roman army was strung out in the sudden desert darkness in unknown country, King Juba's host fell on them from all sides, annihilating the entire force. The chief criminal was not among the dead and his lieutenant threw himself from a cliff in disgrace. King Juba and Petrius went lion-hunting to celebrate their victory.

"Their joy was short-lived. Envoys brought word the general of the Senate had been murdered by traitors from the land called Gift of The River. His head was sent to the tyrant who now ruled in Rome and another army was marching to command surrender and obedience from King Juba and to arrest Petrius for treason...

"King Juba was enraged at the news. He had defeated the Romans once and now he swore they would have to burn every one of his cities and scatter their stones before he would bow to an upstart soldier or give up his best friend to the vengeance of a mock-trial. He ordered his retainers to strike camp and rode to the nearest of his cities…

"Rumours of the King's vow preceded them. When they arrived at the city at dusk, they found the gates closed. From the walls, the voice of a sentry demanded to know who dared approach the city after sunset.

"'Open the gates!' cried the King's herald, 'In the name of the King!'

"'We have no King,' came the reply, 'Nor do we admit strangers who come in darkness. Begone from our gates!'

"Furious, the King himself shouted, 'It is I, King Juba! Open at once or by morning your heads will be spiked on the walls to stand guard until the end of the world!'

"Again came the reply, 'We have no King! Nor do we suffer madmen to loiter at our gates disturbing the peace. Begone before our archers draw their bows or you will surely die!'

"With only a small escort, King Juba knew he could not force the gates. He and Petrius took counsel, deciding to press on through the night to the next city in the kingdom. As they rode through the darkness, Juba described the torments he would devise to punish the city which had denied its King. He would raze the town and divide the spoils among his men. What would not burn would be cast down, no two bricks left standing together. He would deny them the mercy of the sword, but not a soul was to be sold into slavery. Instead, he would have every man, woman and child crucified on the devastated site of their town and left in agony without food, water or shelter, as they had left him. Let jackals gnaw their feet and entrails! Let vultures feast upon their eyes!…

"Though it was mid-day when they arrived at the next city, the fields and farms were deserted and the gates closed. The walls appeared unmanned and their approach was not challenged, so the King's herald had to beat on the gates with the butt of his spear.

"'Open in the name of the King!' he cried. When no reply was forthcoming, the herald climbed the wall and pulled himself over the battlement. Moments later there was a single sharp cry and the body of the herald dropped into the dust before the King's startled horse.

"'You have slain a Royal Herald!' King Juba roared, 'Your lands and your very lives are forfeit!'

"'We have no King,' said a hidden voice from above, 'And thus do we deal with intruders! Begone quickly, or share the fate of your comrade!'

"Withdrawing to a safe distance, King Juba and Petrius saw a dust cloud approaching from the direction they had come. King Juba was certain the riders he had sent to raise his army were bringing warriors to the aid of their King and dispatched a messenger to greet them. But the man came pelting back, shouting it was not the King's host but the Roman cavalry pursuing them. King Juba and Petrius had to ride hard to escape.

"Thus they travelled from town to town, always harried by the relentless Romans and at every city the gates were closed against them and the people said, 'We have no King!' The King became morose and not even a song from Petrius could cheer him. Their retainers began to desert, slipping away shamefully in darkness. At last only one servant remained, a black slave called The Mute because he had never spoken since the day he had been captured as a boy from the green jungles beyond the Great Desert. The King, Petrius and The Mute came at last into the harsh stony country which borders the Sea of Sand. And still they were pursued...

"King Juba did not pause or speak, but rode on into the trackless ocean of sand. Petrius and The Mute rode after him. They crossed the country called The Waters of Death, where demons live in brilliant blue lakes which ever recede and drive men mad with thirst. Finally they came to the inmost place, the land which men of the desert call The Eye of God, saying that only here does God look directly down upon the world, blasting it with His gaze. Nothing would follow them here. Not Romans, not jackals, not even vultures, for The Eye of God shrivels all that lives...

"In the centre of The Eye of God they raised their tents, nibbled the last of their bread and drank all but a few mouthfuls of water. In the awful silence of that night, King Juba and Petrius spoke as friends for the last time. When they embraced and retired to their tents, King Juba called The Mute to him with signs and gestures, giving him to understand he had one final service to perform on the coming day.

"'Then you will be free,' said the King with a contemptuous wave of his hand.

"When The Eye of God opened on the world once more, King Juba and Petrius rose and put on their armour. As they stepped into the already blinding light, Petrius drew his short Roman sword and King Juba the curved scimitar which had been his sceptre as his saddle had been his throne. The friends saluted each other. Then, without a word, their blades crossed and the duel began...

"Despite the pitiless heat and the many wounds they gave

one another, the terrible struggle continued until their shadows were so long on the parched earth it seemed as if two giants strove together there under The Eye of God. The Mute stood watch until the blow no man can parry was struck at last. But the heat and wounds had taken their toll and the victor collapsed beside the vanquished.

"The Mute waited for a time. The King's order had been clear. At last he strode over to the two motionless figures and picked up King Juba's long curved sword. Whirling it once over his head, as The Eye of God closed he plunged it into the heaving breast of the prostrate survivor with a fierce cry.

"He was free! Taking only the flaccid water-skin and the King's long sword, he mounted the strongest horse and fled from The Eye of God...."

The white man's gaze followed the sweep of the long curving blade as it was whipped suddenly away and pointed out across the limitless moonlit waves of sand.

"If you still wish to be free, go now!" hissed The Silent One, "No one will harm or prevent you. You may find your destiny, recover your throne... or perhaps you will find The Eye of God."

The white man tottered weakly to his feet. He peered out into the vacant shimmering sea of sand and trembled. The eyes of the black man were fixed, staring along the extended blade into infinite emptiness. Turning away, the white man began stumbling wearily down the dune toward the camp of chained men. Behind him he heard laughter, like the howling of a mad god, rising through the darkness toward the unblinking moon.

The sun had dropped while I was reading. I was suddenly cold and very tired. Over the North Shore mountains, the moon was already visible in the deepening blue sky. I had no appetite for more beer or food. I felt I had somehow been away for a long time, that it was really much later than the time on the stove clock, really too late to call Laine, as a responsible friend would have done. Too late to get dressed and drive the ten or twelve blocks to her place and show her the story, make her read it, to see what she didn't want to see and her daughter never meant her to see. Too late to betray Lisa's confidence, too late to weigh one act against another and decide which was loyalty, which treason.

The apartment felt so empty I was afraid echoes would rise like ghosts. If I still had a TV and lamps I'd have turned them all on to push back the darkness and silence. Instead, I tip-toed to the bedroom and dived under the quilt, curling into a ball and wishing I was in the back room of Harry's New-To-U with Buzz spooned against my back, Lucky draped snoring and farting over my legs, and the muted soundtrack of some naive apocalypse in the background. I was too whipped to drive across town. I stumbled down the slope of sleep like a slave.

Chapter 15

"Where *have* you been shacking up?"

Laine stormed into my office Friday morning without knocking. At least her badgering tone was light-hearted and she had yet to question me about the incident with Chris, who I heard was having his bandages changed and his wounds bathed by solicitous young models three or four times a day.

"Clients have told me they've called you without getting your machine. You really must remember to turn that thing on when you're out or cave in and wear a pager. I know the fucking things don't accessorize with anything but drug dealer sweats, but in our business, we have to be on-call for twenty-four hour ego-sage…I suppose you've got some tasty young man stashed away in a penthouse with a moonlit jacuzzi…"

I stifled a snort. What would Laine think if she'd seen me, immersed in the old enamel tub, wallowing in a fluffy white cloud of Bert and Ernie Bubble Bath, swilling Black Label from a can, reading a *Wonder Woman* comic and watching *Godzilla,* Jaques Cousteau, Oprah and an old re-run of *Bonanza* while Buzz tinkered with the oily innards of his motorcycle in the back room of New To U? I wasn't about to tell Laine I got forty bucks for my answering machine at the flea market the weekend before.

"I think my machine's going through the Change of Life."

Laine smiled indulgently.

"Alright, be mysterious. But I want all the steamy details over brunch this Sunday. Just the two of us. Mark has a crash deadline on a crucial issue and he's hired a new editor to clean house. Someone I recommended, of course... My place. Noon..."

"Laine, I don't think..."

I didn't know how to tell Laine I was going to be at the flea market on Sunday and not as a browser. Laine wasn't in a listening mood anyway and it immediately became apparent I'd misread her light bantering approach. She leaned over my desk and lowered her voice.

"Seriously, Eve. I have to talk to you, and not just about your private life. I've had major complaints from both clients and staff about your attitude at the office lately. Assaulting a photographer is something I don't want to get into because I know the relationship between models and photographers can easily get inappropriately personal, with mixed signals and misunderstandings, and I know you and Chris are really friends. But when I hear tales about you, of all people, stripping in front of clients, hunky notwithstanding, tossing lingerie out your office window and such... I know I'm not getting the full read here, but I have to assume you've got your knickers caught in your zipper somewhere."

She put up a hand to forestall my attempt to clarify the pantyhose episode. How could I have known the balled hosiery would unroll and drift on the perpetual wind-tunnel breeze up Water Street, my phantom legs spread to the world like a mischievous dragon kite made of sexual ectoplasm, causing two fender-benders, a traffic jam and a minor scuffle between some street people and a client of The Agency, who was now suing a homeless person for assault, according to the *Vancouver Sun* gossip columnist, who'd been sipping his own version of Scotch Broth as lunch for four hours at the Water Street Bistro and witnessed the incident and used it in his column the next day?

Someone, Gail I suspected, since she was known to be the port-in-a-storm for Chris when his companion of an evening turned drunkenly argumentative, menstrual or comatose, had clipped the column and stuck it to the staff noticeboard, with a cc/photocopy to Laine no doubt.

"Since we are friends, after all, and have been for a long time, I think it would be better to talk over brunch, instead of during working hours."

I agreed. I wanted to talk privately too. The pictures Chris had taken of Lisa were something she could treat as a business matter, but the second story Lisa had given me, which seemed to glorify a suicide pact as the highest form of friendship, was something I felt she needed to be aware of as a parent, a mother, however widely she interpreted the definition. The thought exhausted me. Why had Lisa made me her reader, the confidante and custodian of her secret life? Are children like cats, mysteriously attracted to the very people who are afraid of them?

I didn't call Buzz, since I was going directly to the shop from work anyway, as I had every night for the rest of the week since reading Lisa's story. That night I spent shivering and sweating like a fever victim under my quilt. Tossing like a wrestler locked in a cage-match with a huge, brutal opponent I fled from one oppressive anxious dream to another. Half awake, I got up to drain two cold beers in quick belching succession, shivering at the sink, disbelieving the range clock which told me I still had time to shower, dress and go clubbing for an hour or two.

Hoping the alcohol would push my head down deep enough to drown for a few hours, longing for brandy, I fell back into bed only to get up two hours later to pee, stunned and blinking in the bathroom vanity glare, the seat chilling my bum, the lino freezing my feet. Downing glasses of cold water to fight dehydration, back to bed, up in two hours to pee again with a nightmarish sense of *deja vu* shivering in the bathroom, worse than any bender because I knew four tins of beer spread over six to eight hours couldn't possibly do this to anyone.

At dawn I was already up again, sipping strong French Roast and smoking at the kitchen table, wrapped in an old pilled terrycloth robe I only wore on the first days of my period or when I had a cold or flu, watching the sun come up over the North Shore mountains. I watched The Eye of God open on the world before I had a long hot shower and dressed for work.

I called Buzz at noon, asking if I could bring my toothbrush. Something in my voice, some note of desperation peeking out from behind the flirty chit-chat must've tipped him off because he kidded me back with his bogus sales pitch.

"Restorations are our specialty, ma'am. Our guard-dog patrolled premises provides a secure environment in which delicate repairs and refinishing are performed with complete privacy in strict professional confidence…"

"Look, I just want to watch science-fiction videos, eat pasta out of giant salad bowls, drink beer out of wine glasses the size of toilets, get laid and sleep with a big black dog who licks fleas off his balls in the middle of the night."

"I believe we can accommodate your rather unusual needs, ma'am."

"I'll be there around six. Boil some water and pull out the couch."

"What makes you think I folded it back?"

"Is this your way of warning me you haven't changed the sheets?"

"I like the smell of your hair lingering on the pillows. So does Lucky."

"That's the nicest thing anyone's said to me in a long time because I think you really mean it, even though it means you've been sleeping with the dog."

"Yes."

"You're sure you're okay with me invading your space on short notice?"

"Yes."

"Even if it's for more than one night?"

"Yes."

"You really don't mind?"

"No."

"Can I bring dinner?"

"Yes."

"What's with the one-word answers? We haven't known

each other long enough to run out of conversation."

"Just testing a theory that all the important questions in life can be answered like a pogey report. Remember the t-shirts guys used to wear that just said 'Yes Yes Yes No Yes'? It was the sequence of replies you wrote on your UI form every week to qualifiy for benefits. We even got the sequence right. That's a first. Must be fate."

"Life's not that simple…"

"Sure it is. It's just that simple. The rest is small talk. A newspaper editor I worked for years ago used to paralyze the office for hours in the middle of a busy deadline day recounting long amusing stories about his boyhood in Scotland and his career on the amateur stage, his literary friends and political friends, who said what to whom over the third Glenlivet and whatnot. The only one who ever dared interrupt him was this young guy from Montreal who came to work at the paper. After a few minutes of one of these rambles he'd start making this hurry-up gesture with his hand and saying, 'le point, le point,' only you have to say it with a French-Canadian accent so it sounds like a Canada Goose honking, *le pwon, le pwon*. The editor had lived in Montreal and knew it meant, 'shit or get off the pot, asshole.' He found a reason to fire the guy fast."

"But people like to make small talk… They need to. It's a… social lubricant or whatever."

"Sure, as long as they know its the K-Y of conversation, not some grand process of examining the options and developing a strategy for coming to a decision by building a consensus, or some equally inflated fart-noise. That's the brand of bullshit that keeps bureaucrats, psychiatrists and social workers out of foxholes and boards of directors in meeting rooms with comfy chairs and single malt scotch."

"You're a hard man."

His quiet chuckle tickled my ear.

"A cocktail waitress I once served time with used to say, 'A hard man is good to find.'…"

Up to a point, I agreed with her. All the rest of the week I'd slept deeply and restfully on the lumpy pulled out couch at the shop after only a lazy beer or two in lieu of brandy. Even though Buzz and I were on the steep sexual learning-curve new lovers enjoy, with everything getting better and more varied every time we did it, he wasn't some twenty-year-old recruit who needed close order drill every hour or the manual of arms to remind him how to march in step.

Sex seemed to wake him up, infuse him with a relaxed energy. He didn't sleep afterwards but stayed up, fiddling and fixing a dozen things while reading bits of half a dozen books and watching and taping old movies. As soon as he got too absorbed in whatever he was doing to notice, Lucky would sneak off his chair, creep up onto the bed and install himself against my legs and I'd be asleep in an instant. If I did wake up in the middle of the night to Buzz apologizing for having dropped a wrench or video tape or turning up the sound too loud by accident, I'd have a cup of tea, or split a beer with him, chat for a bit and drop off again, no problem, with Lucky warm and vigilant beside me.

As for me, I adjusted to this bizarre parody of conventional domesticity with shocking ease. The shop was like a parallel universe, the fun-house mirror image of the empty perfect apartment I'd fled. There wasn't a utensil, appliance, gadget or widget I didn't possess in multiple variations and, as Buzz predicted, I couldn't even think of uses for half the things on hand. I discovered boxes of clothes, gangster suits and cocktail dresses, blouses from the Fifties with padded shoulders, pullovers, cardigans, enough to open a retro fashion boutique if I felt like it. Yet none of it was mine. I didn't have to possess it, store it, ship it, deal with it at all except to help Buzz sell it or trade it for different interesting stuff. Instead of the heavy responsibility I felt when I looked at my empty perfect apartment, I felt light-footed, dancing in the clogged aisles of New-To-U.

Buzz never asked why I suddenly needed to move in with him. At first I thought he was just waiting for the right moment or for me to tell him. Then I realized he wasn't waiting. He'd given his one-word answer. His faith that my reasons were valid, validated them. That made me want to tell him all the more, but by then I didn't know how to start so I showed him the two stories Lisa had given me to read.

"They're gifts, I guess you'd call them, from a fourteen-year-old girl I met through The Agency."

He read them in the bath, the pages propped on his caddy, a tin of Black Label in the well and a rank Colts cigarillo smouldering in the ashtray. He handed me back the pages and took a long pull on his beer.

"Pretty heavy shit for fourteen. What's she doing modelling if she writes this kind of stuff?"

"Well, it's a little more complicated than that. She's really very beautiful, or will be in a year or so, and she's not actually a model. I should probably have mentioned this girl is deaf. She doesn't hear anything. Hasn't from birth. She doesn't speak, so its kind of neat that her stories are about people telling stories and story-tellers being punished for telling stories people don't want to hear, stories being used almost like instruments of torture in the second one. It being told by a character called The Mute obviously…"

The ripples in the bath stopped.

"She's what?"

"Deaf. Actually she's my boss's daughter. You met her once. My boss, I mean. That was Laine, the first day we met, at the flea market on Terminal Avenue. She bought the dance book from you and I brought it back. You didn't hit it off… She's Lisa's mother."

"Lisa."

He didn't say it like he was trying to memorize her name. He said it quietly, as if he was repeating something he'd heard a long time ago. Then he vaulted out of the tub and towelled off like his skin was on fire.

"Lucky needs a walk."

He and the dog were out the back door while I was still wondering what the fuck I'd said. I trailed my fingers in the bathwater. It was still hot, so I stripped off my loose comfy sweats and lowered myself into the frothy warmth, soaking in his scent hidden under the Sesame Street bubbles.

Chapter 16

Sunday was hot and I was glad for a moment to step into the air-conditioned coolness of Laine's townhouse, a block off Point Grey Road. If Buzz was disappointed by me excusing myself from going to the flea markets, he didn't show it. He'd been very quiet since reading Lisa's stories and once I'd stepped into the back room and caught him with the pages spread out on the workbench. Only Lucky, sitting up in the passenger seat of the van as they drove off, turned his mournful brown eyes questioningly to me as I waved.

"I'll be there when you get back."

I brandished the duplicate key he'd cut for me, another of his sidelines. He learned it, he told me, because he'd always liked the almost masonic secrecy of people who worked with keys and locks and once even sent away for information about becoming a locksmith from an ad on a matchbook cover. When I laughed he told me to watch it because he'd also taken courses in industrial demolition and got his blasting ticket for the same reason. Never used, it was there in his wallet. He showed me.

"Okay. Should we bring back a pizza or something?" He reminded me of a husband asking if he should bring home a quart of milk.

"No. I'll have dinner ready. I'll make you both something special." I was gradually weaning him off convenience foods, though he confessed once, having done justice to my marinated pork chops, that he'd stopped for a nuked Hot Hoagie at the 7-11 on the way home. A craving had come over him, he admitted with a grin.

"Withdrawal. Got that microwave monkey on my back."

Laine had prepared crepes wrapped around delicate white asparagus and thinly shaved ham in a creamy white wine sauce. Given her professed culinary incompetence, this was decidedly ominous. We ate at the kitchen table in cool silence, Laine pensively watching the shirtless brown shoulders of the young men working on the project landscaping, while I gazed at the wide view of English Bay, which made me feel agoraphobic after a week in the bunker-like refuge of the shop. Laine placed her silver Georg Jensen knife and fork together and dabbed at her lips with a celadon coloured napkin.

"Shall we adjourn to the terrace and bag a few rays? Give the boys a treat?"

Laine's one-piece strapless sunsuit, cut high on the hip, might give them a kick, but my own jeans and t-shirt would hardly raise an eyebrow, never mind anything else. Still, I turned down Laine's offer of a bandeau and some cute little shorts.

"I'm fine."

I wasn't. On the blistering deck, I immediately felt like a Fudgsicle dropped on a hot sidewalk. Settled in her lounger with a glass of wine, Laine still seemed reluctant to come to the point. The heat, rich food and wine were making me feel muzzy, almost nauseated.

"Isn't that one a chunk?"

I followed Laine's gaze. A clean-shaven young man, his blonde hair cropped to military shortness, white skin showing red now where beard had masked him, was swinging a mattock with savage force, digging a hole for a waiting shrub whose root-ball was wrapped in wet burlap. The muscles of his arms and shoulders roiled under a fresh sunburn. Large blue tattoos, unrecognizable at this distance, stained his biceps and forearms.

Though he couldn't possibly have heard us, he turned suddenly and smiled at us the way a wolf must curl its lip at rabbits in a box canyon, his pick dangling from one hand like a Viking war-axe. His eyes were tunnels without light at the end. I froze, dropping my wine glass. The sound of it shattering seemed distant, like the sound of windows breaking in a riot blocks away. Laine grabbed my arm.

"My God, what's wrong? You look like you're going to toss your mixed greens, girl. Was it the crepes?…"

Wiping the sweat from his forehead with his arm, the young man whirled and resumed his brutal excavation.

"It's…it's him."

"What?" Laine slammed her own glass down on the terrace table. "Him who? What *are* you talking about?"

I looked down at the turquoise painted deck. "That guy… The one who jumped in front of the car… When we went to the flea market… The one you tried to run down. That's him. I'm sure. Those eyes…"

"Eve…"

"He's had a haircut!" I fought to keep my voice below a scream. "And a shave. But it's him! I know it is!"

Laine tossed the young man a cursory glance and turned back to me, her hand resting reassuringly on my arm.

"Eve? Listen to me. He's a perfectly nice young man. I gave him and his partner a beer, right here on this very terrace yesterday afternoon because it was so hot. That's why he looked over here. He's just curious. Maybe he's even fantasizing that next time I might offer him more than a cold beer, but that's all it is. He's nobody. Just a big strong normal young man, working at a stupid normal job, like thousands of others… You, on the other hand, are becoming very strange lately."

I tried to interrupt, but Laine cut me off.

"Hear me out, please, Eve. This is what I invited you over to talk about. Sort of, anyway…You're never home. At least, you never answer your phone and you don't leave your machine on, if you've had it fixed or whatever. You duck out of the office without leaving a number where you can be reached. When you're in the office, you wear the same outfit days in a row or accessorize like the gypsies have come to town. Your makeup is barely a gesture in the direction of presentability and you seem to think hair was meant only to be tied back in a pony-tail. An elastic band is not a fashion statement, Eve. You miss meetings and return calls with a flippant attitude. I know a big part of the work is just schmooze, but its important schmooze… Now, I don't have any idea who this new man of yours is, but he has to realize…"

I giggled hysterically.

"Yes, you do."

"What?"

"You'll remember him. Remember that book you bought at the Terminal Avenue flea market? The dances of the Sixties book for my housewarming? The guy who didn't want to sell it to you? That's him…And by the way, you paid way too much, Laine. Twice the asking price? He played you. You should've offered half."

Laine went very still for a long moment and I felt something like a chill descend onto the burning deck. I expected her to be flustered, but this was way past that on the scale.

"You mean, that dealer? That…asshole? *Him*?"

"He's not an asshole, Laine. A bit eccentric, even a little weird…"

"He's an utter and total asshole."

Her face was already red and going for purple. I shrugged. In spite of everything, we were old friends and I didn't want to fight with her about someone she knew nothing about.

"Well, if he is, I guess he's my asshole."

Laine controlled her voice with visible effort. The veins in her suddenly ropy neck looked about to pop.

"Apparently he hasn't bothered to tell you he was my asshole first."

It was my turn to sit very still.

"What?"

With an abrupt wave of her arm, Laine winged her glass into the air and off the porch. It landed somewhere, silently, probably in all the bark mulch, which kind of fluffed the dramatic smashing effect she obviously intended.

"You really are a stupid little bitch, aren't you, Eve? That prick you're spreading your legs for is my ex-husband, you stunned cunt! You never met him. You'd gone to Toronto. Couldn't make it back for the wedding. Demands of Matthew's schedule. Script deadlines. Film festival awards. Remember? Well, that's him, or what's left of him! I nearly up-chucked when I recognized him at that flea market, saw what he'd become…"

"My God… Of course… I didn't know, Laine. I mean, you never sent me wedding photos or anything…"

"Oh, so its my fault for not sending you pictures?"

"I only meant, I never knew what he looked like…" Then I stopped apologizing and started to get mad myself. "What he's become actually isn't so bad, you know? He's his own boss. Lives by his wits and doesn't owe anyone anything. Doesn't waste time or money on the kind of pretentious unnecessary shit most men and most career women have to pretend they think is important…"

Laine arched, half-rising out of her lounger.

"That's as may be, Eve. What *you* need to understand is that you're not going to *be* a career woman much longer unless…"

I interrupted her before she could shift into overdrive.

"Laine? Let me make this easy for us both? I resign. Effective immediately. Okay? "

Laine slumped back in her chair, her mouth open wide enough to catch the flies circling my shattered wineglass.

"Have you gone totally fucking nuts?… Eve…"

"It's what I want, Laine. Really. At least, right now. I wasn't a shit-hot agent anyway. You've been carrying me…"

"You're a good teacher and I was teaching you… You would've…"

187

"I don't want to sell people, Laine. Not even their images. I don't want to take young girls and turn them into vapid bimbos to sell toothpaste, tampons or clothes. But I can sell things. Buzz has taught me…"

"Buzz?" Laine said his name as though it was a four-letter word she never used. "That's not his name. His name is…"

"Buzz is his name now."

She changed tacks quicker than the sailors promenading English Bay on their creamy day-sailing sloops, suddenly all earnest concern.

"But how will you live, Eve?… Your apartment. Your things…"

"I'm giving up the apartment and I've sold most of my things." Saying it out loud made it real. "There's nothing left but a single bed I don't sleep in and a few plants. I can get fifty bucks for the bed and the plants will grow anywhere there's a bit of light, water and good drainage. Hey, maybe that's all people really need, Laine, a little minding, the odd drink and good drainage… Anyway, it doesn't matter. I've been staying with Buzz at his shop. He has a second-hand store. We're making out all right at the swap meets and flea markets…"

Laine's voice could have withered silk flowers.

"Let me understand this clearly. You are giving up an apartment in a heritage building that is to die for in this town, to live in a junk shop? You're giving up a glamourous job with a future, to peddle trash with this…this rag-and-bone man, who just happens to be a stray turd I scraped off my shoes years ago? Eve, for Heaven's sake, think! Shake your head, girl!"

I did shake my head, slowly.

"I have thought about it, Laine. I'm happy. I'm not madly

in love with… your ex-husband. Well, not madly anyway. I'm not fucked stupid. I'm just content, for the first time in such a long time. I really am. We have things, Laine. Lots of things. Way more things than you have, but they're not really… Well, I can't explain it to you. It's just that when I'm with him and Lucky, I feel so…easy. Peaceful, for the first time since I was a little girl sitting in my Dad's lap in the big Laz-E-Boy recliner, sucking Cutty Sark scotch off his finger…"

Laine glared at me.

"Lucky?"

"He's a dog. Buzz's dog. Or rather, my dog, because Buzz rescued him for me, but he had to live with Buzz at the shop because… Oh fuck, why am I telling you this? You don't give a shit about any of it. He's just a dog, Laine. A big black sloppy beautiful dog, that's all."

Laine raised an eyebrow, as if I'd just confessed to some bestial *menage a trois.*

"Well, I hope you're not fantasizing about dragging *my* daughter into some cozy reunion with her lost Daddy in a junkyard flea market because I've noticed the unhealthy relationship developing between you and Lisa and I won't have her influenced by losers and their loser attitudes! Do you understand? I won't…"

She started levitating out of her chair, her voice rising from a whisper to a scream like one of those awful method actors who've watched too many Rod Steiger and Al Pacino demo clips in workshops. I decided that was a good moment to take the pictures of Lisa out of my bag and fan them on the table. Laine sagged back into her chair, her jaw slack with shock, as if I'd just head-butted her lycra-flattened gut. Like a hooked fish in the bottom of a boat, she looked like she was trying to speak, but nothing came out.

"Don't panic. She won't be posing for any more of them, or for anything worse Chris might sell to magazines or some child porn website. This is why I hit him, Laine, if you really want to know. I found these. And if you can remember where your ovaries are, on Monday you might want to take some industrial strength Mister Clean to that shit-stain yourself. Or maybe not, since he's an asset of The Agency…"

It was my cue to exit and I made the most of it.

"I've got to go now, Laine. You know? I've never felt comfortable in this place. It epitomizes the Yuppie Scum school of urban interior design. At least the nouveau riche are honest in their belief that good taste is just something you can buy if your chequebook can take the pressure. The crap you surround yourself with takes it to a whole other level, where paying too much money for shit that looks like its been fished out of a dumpster and tossing it into a room with some first editions and genuine antiques is supposed to personalize your space and reflect your eclectic good taste… But you know what? I've been sticking to this ugly very uncomfortable expensive Danish designer deck chair nobody at a flea market would give you ten bucks for after sitting in it for two seconds. Frankly, I wouldn't want to run a garage sale with the crap in this dump. Now, I have to get home and make dinner for Buzz and Lucky…"

Laine exploded out of her chair, a cyclone of sun-block scented gym-toned limbs tanned at the electric beach.

"How dare you! Just listen to yourself, you fucked up little slag! You're running off to live with my fucking ex-husband! A drunk tinker and a dog! Meanwhile, you're having delusions and seeing pyscho killers among the landscape gardeners!" Laine seized my arm and there was no tenderness in her grip now. "Sit down quietly and I'll give you the name of my therapist. You can take a leave of absence from work…" She glanced at the innocently seductive pictures of her daughter. "As for that rat-fucking weasel Chris Newman, when I'm through with him he'll be lucky to be doing shoots for the War Amps Prosthetic Devices catalogue…"

I jerked my arm free. Something in Laine's face, something in it's way as frightening as the mindless rage in the eyes of the young man she'd tried to run down in Surrey that day, reminded me of the expression on the face of the man who had owned Lucky as Buzz led the dog away, a smugness that masked fear, the torturer robbed of one victim, yet certain of another. It was what I had seen behind Matthew's stone-faced look from the porch in Toronto when I got into the airport limousine, the hidden haughty sneer that said 'You'll be back, and I'll make you crawl every inch of the way.' All the nights in my single bed in the abandoned apartment, it wasn't just the brandy that slugged me down into sleep and the hope of a better day tomorrow, it was the memory of that look that turned my hands into claws, unable to dial, and made me forget my own phone number.

"Goodbye, Laine."

"Just listen to yourself, you lame stupid…girl!"

Laine continued to shout after me as I ran down the cedar burl steps to the parking lot, directly toward the young man who stood with the mattock raised above his head, like an executioner without the black hood. I could have turned and made for the flagstone path to the parking area twenty yards away. Instead, I ran straight at him, my fists clenched, head up. I saw him tense, glaring at me and I screamed.

"Get out of my fucking way!"

With a lupine grin, he stepped back, mattock still raised. Like a broad-jumper, I hit the curb at full tilt, sailing past him in the air, my heart a hundred feet high in the wind. Soaring over the bark mulch meridian, I hit the parking lot running, hearing the mattock thuck into the defenseless earth behind me.

Chapter 17

Buzz and Lucky and I had a barbecue picnic in the alley, steaks grilled outside the back door of the shop on a near new Hibachi Buzz picked up at a garage sale. I made french fries in a West Bend deep-fryer I found in the course of my explorations of the shop. Later that evening, when Lucky finished grinding the last shreds of meat off the bones, we drove in the van to my apartment to collect my plants. Two indoor weeping figs, a couple of jade plants, the inevitable diefenbachia and a pepper plant were the only living things, almost the only things still there, odd remnants of an unimaginative botanical garden. Buzz said he'd pick up my bed during the week. We could get maybe seventy-five bucks for it at the shop or in the Buy & Sell, probably more than we'd get at the flea market.

Buzz carried the last of the plants down to the van. I stood for a moment in the empty living room and looked around. I smiled as I switched off the light.

"Now it's perfect."

In the dark empty room, the unexpected electronic twitter of the phone was loud and frightening. I picked it up carefully.

"Hello? Is this…?"

The unfamiliar male voice gave my number correctly.

"Yes."

"I'm very sorry to bother you, but I have sort of a problem here." He sounded genuinely concerned. "I just got home and, well, I found this beautiful young girl passed out on my porch. I brought her inside and put her on the couch, but I can't wake her up and I honestly don't know what to do. I don't want to just call the cops and maybe get her in trouble or something… I looked in her purse. Maybe I shouldn't have, but I wanted to find some ID or something with a number I could call. All I found was a piece of paper with your phone number on it. I'm really sorry to trouble you…"

I panicked, trying to think who it might be. One of my girls, my clients, the ones whose interests I was supposed to protect, whose careers I was supposed to guide, drunk or coked out, stunned by a dose of some horse tranquillizer passed off as Extasy at a downtown rave or squirt of Rophynol into her drink in a nightclub.

"What does she look like? Doesn't she have any identification at all?"

Still quiet and concerned, the invisible voice sank to a whisper.

"I thought you might tell me… Do you think it would be alright if I pulled down her pants?"

I took a deep breath and bit my lip, keeping my voice even.

"I think you should go over to the sink first…"

"Yesssss?…"

"And stick your sad, pathetic tiny prick down the garburator and turn it on, you shit-gobbling toad."

I slammed down the phone. As I was closing the door of the apartment, it began to ring again. Laughing, I locked the door behind me and skipped down the stairs to the waiting van.

It wasn't until we were sprawled on the pull out couch in the shop back room, the bath we would share drawn, candles lit, Lucky snoring and farting at our feet, fresh tins of Black Label balanced on our chests as we watched the video of the restored original print of *Casablanca*, that I finally said what had to be said. There was a lull in the onscreen action. Sydney Greenstreet, fat and fezzed as Mr. Ferrari, proprietor of the seedy flyblown Blue Parrot bistro, was advising Mr. and Mrs. Victor Lazlo to consult his business rival Rick Blain about the letters of transit, unaware of the secret relationship between Rick and Ilsa.

"You should have told me you were Laine's ex-husband."

Buzz tensed for a moment, then sagged, more stoic than Bergman confronted by her lover about the marriage she'd neglected to mention.

"How? When? I didn't know who you were or what your relationship with Elaine was. It's funny, because I know she must have told me about you, her friend who was married to the famous writer. All she talked about were the rich and famous people she knew. She probably even showed me your picture. How much attention do you think I paid to shit like that? Sure, I figured out who you were pretty quick, from seeing you with her, from what you said about your husband. But what was I supposed to say? It's been almost ten years since I've seen or heard from Elaine. I was as unpleasantly surprised to see her as she was to see me. It was just an accident. That's all it would have been, but then you had to come back with that damn dance book. And you started calling me, asking me to help you sell things. I didn't call you…"

I took a pull on my beer and nodded.

"No. You didn't. You made me feel like a real flea market groupie. A second-hand slut. One of those depraved girls who steals people's car radios and old discarded furniture from backyards and alleys just so they can hang out with junk dealers…"

He tried to smile through a tired sigh.

"I knew when you brought that dumb little book back there was something special about you, but you were playing on a team I got cut from a long time ago. I just wanted it to be clear that I don't play in that league anymore. I won't ever wear a custom-tailored suit, or have a corner office, or tell anybody I want a report or the sales numbers 'asap' ever again. I'll never ream out a waiter about the doneness of the veal chop, or the vintage of the cabernet, or the temperature of the chardonnay ever again either. There's a lot of things I won't do ever again and those are just the little ones… Shit, even in this racket some people take a kind of creative approach when it comes to the provenance of their merchandise. They usually go upscale and become dealers in 'antiques and collectibles.' I don't ever want to be anything but a second-hand dealer who makes a small honest profit. I don't want to move to a better location on South Granville or in Kits. I don't want to open a second store in Whistler and commute in a Jeep Grand Cherokee. I don't want my shit smelling of any of Umberto's restaurants. I'm a junkman and I'm not going to change. Not for anybody. Not even for you. You might as well know…"

I sat up and took a longer pull on my beer.

"Spare me the manifesto. I knew everything I needed to know about you when you traded a near-new Sony portable for a dog you didn't want. It doesn't matter how you feel about me in the long run, but what I do want to know now is what you're going to do about Lisa."

The empty Black Label tin imploded slowly and noisily in his closing fist.

"Okay. Tell me. Just what is it you think I should do? I haven't even seen her for six or seven years and then my custody visits just upset her. I don't know her… She doesn't know me…"

"Maybe it's time you got to know her…and time she got to know you."

I put up my hand to smooth the hackles I sensed invisibly rising. Even Lucky opened one eye and tensed almost imperceptibly at the foot of the bed.

"I'm not going to do anything. Laine, Elaine, made it very clear I'm not to have any further contact with her daughter and I don't have any right to meddle in Lisa's life. Or yours, as far as that goes. You took me in when I needed to get out of something I was trapped in. You jimmied the back door, pried open the leg-hold trap, and let me run. I'm not sure what I've escaped to yet, or where I'm going…"

"Knowing where you don't want to be, having the guts to walk out in the middle of a bad movie, is a good start."

On the muted screen, Bogart was giving the letters of transit to Ilsa and Victor Lazlo, about to begin his famous speech about the problems of two people not amounting to a hill of beans in this crazy world and how they'd always have Paris. One of the great romantic scenes in modern film and I suddenly saw what a transparently bogus bit of wartime propaganda it really was.

It was the problems of the whole crazy world that didn't amount to a hill of beans, compared those too brief, too rare moments of genuine affirmation which occur between human beings. If Rick had an ounce of sense, he'd have scooped Ilsa, used the visas and vanished, leaving the Victor Lazlos, the Major Strassers and all the other dimestore demagogues so willing to sacrifice other people's lives for their ideals to shoot it out on the Main Street of history.

"I just want you to know how much I appreciate everything you've done for me." Groping in my handbag, I found the folded pages of the stories Lisa had given me and handed them to Buzz. "Here. These are the most precious things I own now because they're very special to Lisa and she chose to share them with me. I'm giving them to you. I don't think she'd mind. They're second-hand, but you're used to that. Now you can stop sneaking them out of my bag to re-read them every time I'm out of the room."

His smile was grateful, but still a bit wan. I rolled off the bed and shook Lucky's leash, galvanizing him. He was at the back door wagging his whole spine before I shoved my sockless feet into my clammy sneakers.

"I'm taking Lucky around the block for a pee patrol. Do your bedtime reading while I'm out and put on another video. No more Bogart, unless it's *The Maltese Falcon*. I like his big final speech, when he tells Mary Astor he's turning her over to the cops even though he loves her, because at bottom he knows she's a heartless bitch. Let's watch *War of the Worlds* or

The Time Machine instead, something cheerful to get you in the mood."

I didn't think it was possible to slip from one world to another as smoothly as a diving submarine, but that was exactly what happened. I vanished from my own life like a set of wet footprints that ends at blank wall, then dries and disappears, in a Sherlock Holmes mystery starring Basil Rathbone. I'd left the phone number of New-To-U with Gail as a sort of forwarding address, but nobody called except her. There was no point in feeling bitter. For the clients, The Agency was still their agent, Laine was still in charge and there was no percentage in showing any kind of sympathy or solidarity with someone who was Out in every sense of the word bar one. As for Gail, she only wanted to pump me for details of my tragic fall to retail on coffee break or whisper to curious clients at her desk, the All-Seeing All-Knowing Madame Gail. When I wouldn't purge the ghastly details of my break with Laine, she suddenly pleaded a busy switchboard and I laughed into her ear.

"It's probably Chris, calling from downstairs on his cell, too whipped to make the climb. The girls have stopped being impressed by his war wound and he's looking for one last sympathy fuck before the bandages come off. Better answer it, dear."

The bitch hung up on me. Imagine.

Buzz picked up my bed, the last of my things from the apartment. It was for sale in the shop and my plants had replaced the tangle of tools in the front window, thriving perversely in the stale atmosphere that always seems to emanate from an accumulation of second-hand things. He dropped off the apartment keys with the building manager and left no forwarding address. The manager seemed upset, he told me. He thought the lease was being broken, but the apartment had been sublet under the table so many times he was no longer sure how to contact the nominal tenant. No one had moved out of the building without moving in a suitable tenant in so long he couldn't recall how to handle the situation.

Buzz told me the phone rang while he was moving the bed. My heart seized briefly at the memory of that last horrible call, the soft sincere sickening voice oozing out of the dark.

"Did you answer it?"

"Why would I? I knew it wasn't for me."

I hugged him fiercely. Slightly bewildered, he went back to working on his motorcycle, Lucky patiently studying his every move, while I sipped a beer and marvelled at the perfection of a man who wouldn't answer a ringing phone because he knew the call wasn't for him.

"Your conspiracy theory is wrong."

He snorted.

"Which one?"

"The one about beautiful people being evidence that aliens are among us. It's not them. It's really you."

"Nice try, but no rum-soaked wine-dipped cigarillo for you. If it was me, kid, I'd be Michael Rennie, wear a cool mylar and foil-wrap jumpsuit, drive an interplanetary M-60 tank. Read the Galactic Riot Act and introduce my big silent enforcer pal Gort. A little 'Klaatu barada nikto' and this fucked up asteroid would get the kind of serious bylaw enforcement it needs."

For the next few weeks, I was too busy to brood. Despite

his declared antipathy to running a boutique business, my efforts at re-organizing the shop were met with cantankerously expressed satisfaction. Every time he bitched about actually being able to find things for a change, I pointed to the cash drawer and observed that when customers could find things they tended to buy them, thus providing us with more capital to buy things to sell. We hadn't got to repainting or stripping and refinishing the old distressed wooden floors, but New-To-U was cosier, more inviting and word was obviously getting around it was a good place to shop for bargains.

Having me around meant customers no longer encountered a locked door with the 'Back Whenever' sign in the window when Buzz was off on his scavenging forays to the Sally Ann or thrift stores, the trap-line of flea markets, auctions, garage sales and charity drop-offs he worked in the old blue van. It made covering the markets easier too. While I minded a table or booth, Buzz could keep the shop open and catch up on the small appliance repairs. We both loved kitchen appliances from the Forties and early Fifties, but not for the same reasons. While I admired the retro design of stainless steel toasters, blenders and percolators, the heavy Bakelite of Mixmasters, he loved what was inside, loved bringing these dead things back to life.

"These things are solid. Like mass-produced furniture from the first half of the 20th century. It stands up. Not like the stapled-together pressboard shit they charge thousands for now. These things represent the brief failed marriage of craftsmanship and mass production. Like most marriages, it didn't last. Disputes over money are at the root of most divorces. Planned obsolescence cited as co-respondent and home-wrecker. If you build a car that lasts sixty years, how're you going to sell them a new car every two years? Just toss it and get a new one. New house, new car, new toaster, new wife, new life."

He tended to get ranty when he worked in the back shop and I felt it was better for him to get out to the markets and deal with people on the weekends. Lucky went with him sometimes, but mostly he stayed in the shop with me, mascot and unlikely but effective watchdog, making friends with customers, but snarling at malodorous dumpster divers deranged into thinking a shopping cart full of garbage was priceless treasure or punks who unloaded luxury sedan stereos from the trunks of Japanese compacts exploding with rap tunes.

I thought about Lisa often, but stifled my urge to meddle. Buzz had an old poster tacked to the wall in the back room. He told me it had come home, because he'd bought it from this shop years before when he was a bartender at The Blue Parrot, the cocktail lounge of the old hotel which used to be just around the corner where a big spike of apartments stands now, its only memorial the strange salvaged blue neon parrot we use as a nite-lite. The poster shows hands demonstrating the sign language of the deaf. One night I rolled over, half awake. The original *King Kong* was on TV, Faye Wray shrieking in the palm of the giant ape tragically in love with her. Buzz was looking at the poster and his fingers were speaking a silent language I didn't understand.

Chapter 18

The next time I saw Laine was on television. Late one evening I was relaxing in the big tub, grazing on popcorn hot from an AirBlast machine, watching Lon Chaney turn into the Wolfman, one of those movies filmed in San Francisco just so the cops and criminals could chase each other down the city's roller-coaster hills, mini-subs exploring the Titanic wreck and the eleven o'clock news, all with the sound off and Spike Jones *Greatest Hits* on the turntable. Suddenly I found myself staring at a head-shot Chris had taken of Laine not long after they met. It wasn't until they cut to live coverage, police cruisers and the ambulance, red lights pulsing like illuminated wounds, that I recognized Laine's townhouse complex and grabbed the remotes from the bath caddy, cut off Spike Jones in the middle of "Cocktails for Two" and cranked up the sound.

"…found brutally bludgeoned to death in her Kitsilano

home this evening… Police have a thirty-one-year-old man in custody in connection with the incident and charges are expected to be laid tomorrow morning…"

The camera cut to a close-up of a police car. Hands manacled behind him, the suspect struggled in the collective grip of huge Vancouver police officers. A cheap wind-breaker had been awkwardly pulled up to hide his head, but as they hustled him into the back of the car, he thrashed, snarling, spitting, kicking and trying to bite his captors, his face contorted beyond recognition. For a moment, I saw his eyes, but they were only the eyes of any madman, anywhere. Then a policeman blocked the lens with one hand, eagerly reaching for his night-stick with the other.

I threw up into the bath.

"Jesus! What…?"

Buzz stared at the TV while the anchor man repeated the lead story with the photo of Laine superimposed behind him, then he cut all the TVs off with a flick of a remote. Sound and pictures vanished like a magician's illusion.

"Eve? Are you…?"

I threw up again, all over him this time. He ran a cloth under hot water and cleaned me up as I stood beside the tub, shaking uncontrollably. Wrapping me in a blanket, he held me on the bed while Lucky snuggled against me on the other side, licking my hand, until I finally stopped shaking.

"What about y-you? S-she was y-your…"

He shrugged patiently.

"Several lifetimes ago… Look, I wouldn't wish a death like that even on someone I hated and I didn't hate Elaine. Not for long, anyway. Then I didn't feel anything one way or another. I can't pretend I feel much of anything now, except sorry she died like that."

"But you had a child with her! You still have! What about Lisa? Her mother's just been murdered. What if she was there? What about her, you smug heartless fucker?"

Churning with rage, I started punching him in the face as hard as I could, as hard as I'd swung the film bag at Chris Newman. He blocked most of my punches calmly, taking one that made his nose bleed a trickle. Finally I ran out of steam.

"You done?"

I fell back on the bed.

"I'm done."

"Okay." He got up and wiped the thread of blood from his nose on his sleeve. "I have to call Elaine's mother. I'm not sure what I'm going to say…See if there's anything I can do."

I sat up.

"Do you want me to do it? Elaine and I…were friends and I know Lisa."

"And I'm her father, as you pointed out… I'll do it."

Leaving me curled up with my arms around Lucky, he drained and cleaned the tub and made me a cup of hot Chicken In A Mug. Then he went out into the darkened shop to use the phone at the desk near the door. I drank the salty instant chicken broth, listening to the quiet murmur of his voice in the outer dark. When I felt able to get up, he caught me under the arms coming back from the shop and hefted me back into bed.

"Lisa's at her Grandma's, like always. She was doing her homework, so she didn't see the six o clock news, but she's been told. Elaine's mom sounds like she's holding steady right now. She's a tough lady, but she's been dealing with cops and all that shit and the shock will hit her in a few hours. Someone should be there. I asked her if she wanted me to come over and she said yes. I don't know why she'd want to see me after all this time, but she does. Will you be alright here with Lucky?"

"Of course."

"I've left the number by the phone out front."

"Get going. I'm alright. I'm pretty tough too."

"Yeah. You are… Oh, she said something a little odd. She asked me if I knew a woman named Eve, a friend of Elaine's. Apparently Lisa's told her Grandmother quite a bit about you…"

I started up off the bed.

"I should come with you then… In case Lisa…"

"Tomorrow. Lisa's asleep now and she should stay that way. Doctor gave her a sedative. Other people have been calling since it happened. Someone named Amanda. When Elaine's mother asked her if she knew how to contact Eve, Amanda said she's been looking for you too. You might want to call her when you feel up to it."

As I heard the old van rattle down the alley, I pulled on my jeans and one of Buzz's warm sweatshirts. I lit a cigarette, my first in days and found my almost tossed memo book at the bottom of my purse. She picked up on the first ring, like you do when the phone makes you jump, afraid it will wake someone sleeping.

"Amanda? It's Eve."

"Are you alright, Eve? Where are you?" The familiar rich voice was subdued. Amanda wasn't projecting, over-dramatizing in the way that used to make my scalp hurt.

"I think so. I'm alright, more or less, now. I was watching the news…"

"Yes. It's dreadful. Worse than they made out, apparently. Poor Michael. He was supposed to drop by her place this afternoon, right about the time it happened, but he was delayed at a shoot at some golf club and the police were there when he arrived. He went completely frag. He's asleep now, I hope, but it took a lot of Valium. Are you sure you're alright? Where are you?"

"I'm okay. I'm sorry I called so late. I'm not even sure why I called. I don't know what to say…"

"No. Neither do I. It's all so senseless, so savage and random, somehow, that there just isn't anything *to* say. That's the trouble, isn't it?"

"Yes." I felt oddly close to Amanda for the first time, reluctant to hang up, but at a loss for anything to say that might fill up the hollow silence of the phone.

"Eve?… It's none of my business, but have you heard from Matthew?"

"Matthew?"

"Your husband."

"Oh, right… No… Why?"

"It's just that, the other night, when Laine…" She forced herself to continue. "When she was over, she said Matthew had been calling her, trying to get in touch with you. You didn't give her your new number or an address or anything…"

"I left a number with Gail, though she may have flushed it with a tampon."

"Maybe she meant you hadn't actually given it to her personally. All she said was that she wasn't Matthew's agent and she wasn't going to run his errands."

"I'll call him. Thanks for telling me… I'd better let you go."

"Eve?… I just want to say, whatever it is you've found, or

whatever it is you're doing, I wish you the very best of luck."

"I know. Thank you, Amanda. Good luck to you too. You and Michael."

I put the phone down softly.

I searched my memory for my Toronto phone number and dialed. I knew he would be awake, keeping to his late-night writing schedule.

"Matthew?"

"Hello? Evie?... Where have you...?"

"What do you want, Matthew? Why have you been trying to get in touch with me?"

"I called Laine. She told me you're not working for her anymore. My lawyers say you don't answer your mail. Your phone's disconnected. Does this mean you might be thinking of coming home or...?"

"I am home... Just tell me what you want."

"Well, I...well, I want to know what you're planning to do about this agreement, I guess. I want to know what to do about your things. If you're thinking of..."

He didn't sound as sure of himself as he had a moment before, when he was sure I was crawling away from the burning wreckage of my attempt at independent flight.

"Give them away. Or hold a garage sale, Matthew. Better yet, get a table and sell them at a flea market."

"A what?" His precise intimidating tone faded into groping confusion. "Look, you spent years and a lot of money collecting those..."

"I've got enough things to deal with right now, Matthew."

"But these things were very important to you and I don't want to be responsible... Look, where are you, anyway?"

"I'm in a junk shop."

"A what?"

"A second-hand store. The kind of place I used to drag you through looking for bargains or priceless antiques under coats of pastel enamel. I'm living in a junk shop."

There was a long, exasperated, satisfying silence before he spoke again.

"Eve, why are you living in a junk shop?"

"Well, you could say I'm a partner, I guess. That's why I don't care what you do with those things, Matthew. I just don't have room for them right now and by the time the freight and storage charges are paid, I won't turn enough of a profit on them to make it worth the trouble."

"You don't want them? You'd just…sell them?"

"That's right."

There was another silence.

"Eve? Are you…involved with someone?"

"You could just say I'm a partner."

"Is this somebody you think you love, or what…?"

"Let's just say I'm a partner in something and leave it at that."

"If that's how you want it."

Stiff and formal again, sulking because he couldn't control the conversation, but I didn't care anymore.

"Send the papers to my parents, Matthew. I'll sign them and send them back as fast as I can. Goodbye."

"But…"

"Goodbye, Matthew."

The moment I put down the phone I realized I hadn't told him about Laine.

Chapter 19

The *Vancouver Sun* published the name of the man who murdered Laine when charges were laid. It meant nothing to me. Neither did the grainy newspaper photo of the clean-shaven close-cropped defendant, his tattoos hidden by a stiff new off-the-rack suit his lawyer, a prominent criminal attorney named Doug Williams, had obviously bought for him. It was strange. I recognized Doug Williams because he was a well known bachelor about town who liked the high-profile night life and high-profile cases involving drugs and murder among the various Russian and Punjabi gangs. He'd even represented Jack Morrison on a weapons charge when he was a cab-driver, years ago. Yet I didn't recognize his client, who had supposedly killed my friend. I thought about going to the police with the story of the incident at the Surrey flea market, but since I couldn't positively identify him they'd probably think I was just some sexually paranoid woman, as loony as Laine herself thought I was.

So the Crown Prosecutor never asked if he had been in Surrey on a Sunday some months before the murder or had attempted hijacking a black Porsche. Doug Williams never suggested in his defense presentation that the murder victim had previously tried to run his client over with an expensive German sports car. It occurred to me that even if he was actually the same deranged hitch-hiker we'd nearly clipped in Surrey, it was quite possible he didn't recognize Laine specifically as the arrogant bitch who tried to squash him like a bug on the windshield of her luxury sports coupe.

But he *had* killed her. He didn't deny it. The paraded facts of Laine's death as they were reported in the newspapers seemed to have occurred somewhere else, distant as the dateline on a news story about an atrocity committed in some country of the imagination inhabited by people descending into savage class warfare or tribal ethnic cleansing.

Maybe Laine was right all along. Lots of young men out there had tattoos, shaved off beards and got haircuts to get jobs they didn't really want and were never going to be the kind of men Michael pretended to be in ads and commercials for cars and cologne, shirts and whisky, suits and cigars. Unbranded, they couldn't tell a Jaguar from a Porsche, a snifter of X.O. cognac from a shot of cherry brandy or an Old Port Tipped from a Cohiba. A faded Tommy Hilfiger sweatshirt from the thrift store bin was just a warm shirt which happened to have a name and a faint yellow mustard stain on the chest. The near-new Nikes found in the dumpster with a thick reeking fudge of dogshit wedged in the treads were just a perfectly good pair of shoes some asshole could afford to be too particular to clean up with a popsicle stick and hot water.

But somewhere inside they knew their cars always had bearings run to ratshit filings and seals blown like faulty condoms by careless pre-owners. Their basement suites, apartments and trailers, even their houses had always been trashed, the carpets pissed on by the cats and dogs of previous tenants, or puked on by the tenants themselves. They didn't have to be told to walk a mile in anyone's shoes. Theirs always carried the faint stink of other feet and their clothes had the exfoliated flakes of unfamiliar skin embedded in the fibres.

Their women had always loved someone else, been fucked and impregnated and raped and sodomized and beaten and finally discarded by someone else, and someone else before him. They knew it and it made them hate everything new and clean and expensive that flaunted itself from every magazine, billboard, store window and TV station twenty-four hours a day, seven days a week year in and out. It turned them into lone monsters, trapped in a maze whose glossy ephemeral surfaces were elusive, harder to penetrate than stone.

Despite the language barrier, Buzz and I each tried to explain this to Lisa in different ways, so she wouldn't go through life wondering what her mother had done to make someone hate her enough to kill her. I'd been nervous enough initially just about how she would react to seeing the father who had pretty much abandoned her for most of a decade turn up with me, her murdered mother's friend. If she found it strange, she didn't let on, but then her handicap made it easy for her not to let on anything more than she wanted to. We began by spending time with her separately at first, so she could get used to us both being around before having to see us as a couple.

It was harder for Buzz. He had more ground to cover, so many lost years to make up for, his absence all the space and time of her short life to atone for while he struggled to make some kind of sense out of what had happened to her mother with her. Not long after the story finally dropped from the headlines, when every one of Laine's clients and acquaintances had milked every column-inch, photo op and sound-bite from their association with the victim, he came back from spending the day at the Vancouver Aquarium with Lisa, fell on his back across the unmade pulled out bed and lit one of the ultra mild cigarettes I was using to wean myself off the weed.

"Jesus, you'll hyperventilate, bust a gut and die trying to suck a decent drag out of one of these things long before cancer gets you." He snapped the filter off the end and dropped it in the ashtray. "I miss these things… I think I'll take them up again, now they're so unpopular. Cigarette smoking is the last bastion of passive-aggressive rebellion."

I pulled a tin of Black Label from the bar fridge under the workbench, cracked it and stood it on his chest.

"How was Lisa today? At least the publicity frenzy seems to be fading…"

He sighed heavily, almost knocking over his beer. Catching the can, he sat up, groped in the pocket of his multi-zippered Korean War flying jacket and tossed me some folded sheets of paper with a title written in a hand I recognized.

"We looked at fish all afternoon. She likes the Aquarium. She knows fish don't make any sounds, so she doesn't have to pretend to be reacting to stuff she doesn't hear. We had a long look at the stuffed Coelocanth, that prehistoric monster they dragged up off the coast of Africa ten thousand years after it was supposed to be extinct. When I dropped her off at her

Grandma's, she took this out of her bag and stuck it in my pocket as she got out of the car. You gave me two of her stories, so I'm returning the favour. I read it in a bar, where I actually steadied my nerves with two vodkas that made me very tired. I don't know what it means, but I think she's handling this whole thing better than we are."

I unfolded the pages and read the hand-written title. *The Monster.*

Theseus had no fear of the Labyrinth, though it was said that not even its own architect could escape it. Theseus knew its convoluted secrets could be unravelled as easily as a ball of string. It was the Minotaur that terrified him. The brutality and blood-lust of the Monster were legendary even in its own time, when the appetite of the Gods for the ambrosia of human suffering was well known. Theseus dreaded the moment of confrontation with that divine monstrosity.

When they were cast into the Labyrinth, Theseus became separated from his companions. Some despaired, threw themselves down and refused to stir, preferring to await their fate rather than seek it. Others abandoned the group in the hope of escaping its collective fate or to pursue futile personal quests for an outlet from the impenetrable maze.

Too soon Theseus found himself alone in the oppressive silence. He had expected to hear the screams of outraged maidens and the cries of murdered youths. Worst of all, he had anticipated the ominous bellowings of the Monster itself, but he heard nothing. The silence was broken only by the occasional distant shriek of surprise as two of his fellow victims encountered one another at a turning and fled in opposite directions, each mistaking the other for the object of their mutual fear.

Puzzled, Theseus wandered for some time in the warren of

the Minotaur, breathing the mustiness of an ancient cave which already permeated the dungeon contrived by the architect of the King. At last he entered one of the larger chambers fed by the network of narrow passages and was forced to stop. The ball of string he had unravelled like an aimless spider had been payed out to the end. He sat down on a pile of loose stones broken away from the ceiling of the chamber. Everywhere in the tunnels and alcoves he had noticed heaps of rubble. Mounds of crumbled masonry and splintered shoring blocked some passages completely. Already the famous Labyrinth was being reclaimed, absorbed by the earth from which it had been carved, like the twined initials of lovers absorbed by the regenerating bark of a tree.

His fear gave way to the boredom that follows prolonged tension. He had fallen into an idyllic reverie, a daydream, when he suddenly sensed he was no longer alone. He realized that for some time he had been aware of another breathing, deeper, but in perfect rhythm with his own. Panic twisted in his stomach and pounded at his temples.

The Minotaur stood at the mouth of a tunnel directly before him. In the faint light from the overhead shafts which cunningly ventilated the maze, Theseus saw the tall powerful body, muscles tense and quivering, surmounted by the horrible horned head, in all its monstrous divinity. He wanted to scream, to run, to die, but his whole being refused to obey him.

The Minotaur raised its gigantic hands. Paralysed with fear, Theseus gaped as it came closer, knelt before him, and he felt the huge arms encircle his fragile mortal neck. The Minotaur slowly lowered its enormous head, as if to whisper some ultimate secret in Theseus' ear. Then, with a shudder, it began to weep abjectly on his shoulder.

How long they remained that way, Theseus could not tell. In

time the Monster ceased its sobbing and began to speak. At first, Theseus could hardly credit the sounds for speech. Deformed and awkward with disuse, the tongue of the Minotaur mangled the language of men as savagely as he had mutilated their bodies. Gradually Theseus was able to grasp a word here and a phrase there of the Minotaur's tale.

The Minotaur begged Theseus not to be afraid and implored him not to try to flee. It had come, it explained, resolved to kneel as a supplicant before the first of the intended victims it encountered. It then began a long recitation of its unnatural conception, accursed birth, dreary youth in a dungeon nursery while the Labyrinth was under construction. There followed an account of a bestial existence in the maze, driven by starvation and hatred of humankind to comb the endlessly meandering corridors for the sacrificial victims which provided the only sustenance.

As the years passed, the Minotaur's hatred turned to pity. Time and again he approached his fellow prisoners in friendship, seeking to calm their fears and make common cause with them, but always they fled from him in horror. Was it not more merciful, he asked, to spare them the agonies of terror and starvation by granting them a swift end? And was it not right and just that he should survive, he who was strong enough to endure and perhaps even to conquer the Labyrinth?

He knew the maze and its Monster must have become a byword for cruelty and barbarity throughout the world. If people could be moved by the injustice of the sacrifice decreed by an evil king, could they not be moved by the injustice of his own plight? What was he, after all, but another innocent victim of the greeds and lusts of men and women and the frivolous anger of the Gods?

In the darkness and loneliness of years he had nursed his

plan. All he needed was the word of a single one of his supposed victims to act as his spokesman and guarantor of his good intentions. Would Theseus be the one? Surely he would. He must!

Through it all, Theseus neither spoke nor moved. The Minotaur continued, now in a grateful tone as though all he wished for had already been granted. He understood there could never truly be a place for him in the society of men. His hideous deformity and cannibal reputation would always be horrible to many. Still, was it too much to ask that he be permitted to retire to a secluded cottage somewhere near the sea, where he could admire the freedom of the birds, listen to the whisper of the waves which touched all the shores of the world, smell fresh grass and the scent of wild herbs on the wind, a place where he might never again know hunger and screams, darkness and cold unyielding stone?

Perhaps Theseus might even visit him from time to time, bringing such companions as would not be revolted by his presence, and they would walk over the hills and along the shore and share cups of wine around a bright warm fire in the evening.

Theseus' perch on the pile of stones had become intolerably uncomfortable. Shifting his weight slightly, he put a hand down to steady himself. His fingertips encountered a shard of flint, sharp and heavy as the head of an axe. For a moment, he looked down at the huge bowed head resting gently on his shoulder, the nape of the neck exposed, and felt something like pity.

Then his cry of triumph echoed through the Labyrinth and out into the world.

Folding the pages, I put them carefully aside and leaned forward, laying my head on his shoulder, feeling the draft from the open back door on the nape of my neck like a cool hand. He didn't shift, but sat still and steady as stone.

Chapter 20

I saw Michael once more, by accident, on the long walking path atop the Fraser dike near Steveston in Richmond. I was taking Lisa and Lucky for a walk while Buzz visited a liquidation warehouse nearby. Lisa brought our old dragon kite, the one I'd bought on a whim when we played hooky together, and she dashed ahead, the kite rising on the steady reliable river breeze like a living spirit escaping the bonds of earth.

I almost didn't recognize him. Sniffing and dawdling, Lucky and I overtook a straggling trio, the man moving with the awkward solicitude that is the mark of the stepfather or father on a custody weekend. The little boy broke away and promptly ran back to the bounding Lucky, who licked his face, provoking a squeal of delight.

"Doggie!"

"Mustn't play with strange doggies…"

I could hardly believe it was Michael. The much-photographed face was unshaved, the athletic body buried in an old duffel coat and sweatpants. A portrait of the harried suburban father. In turn, he gaped at me.

"Eve?…What are you doing here?"

"Walking my dog, obviously. He's very gentle with kids, by the way."

We sauntered along together for a while, watching Amanda's kids romp with the big dog ahead of us, but there didn't seem to be anything to say. Michael, who I'd once listened to in rapt fascination as he held forth about Jaguars, nineteenth century engravings, English watercolours and the proper method of cooking Basmati rice, was a bore. Watching the kids nervously, he talked about the weather, like a polite Englishman in a lineup for the bus. Only once, he tried to say something about Laine, but his beautiful face crumpled so pitifully I put my hand over his mouth.

"Michael, don't… There's nothing to say. It's a beautiful sunny day, late in the year. A gift. Let's just walk and enjoy it."

"Amanda and I are going to be married in the spring."

He blurted it out like a man confessing to high treason with a mixture of guilt and defiance.

"That's wonderful. Congratulations. She needs you and so do the kids…And you need them, Michael."

He sighed deeply, conspicuously relieved.

"Yes, I do. It's hard for me to understand… I mean, you think you've made it. You think you're strong. Self-contained. You think you control your life and have everything in it arranged just the way you want it, like furniture arranged in a room. You have almost everything you want and what you don't have, you expect to get soon. Then one day, something happens and you look around and it's all just…furniture. I don't know… You suddenly find yourself standing in a parking lot beside your Jag XJS coupe with its two leather bucket seats, no room for luggage bigger than an overnight bag, envying all those poor bastards you used to pity, with their mini-vans and station wagons full of screaming kids in child safety seats, going home to the lawns they have to mow and their crippling mortgage payments…It doesn't make sense. You have everything, but your life means nothing. They have nothing but debts and obligations, but their lives *mean* something. They're important, not just to someone, but to so many people, in so many ways. They're needed…"

"Maybe they're even happy, Michael." I put my hand on his shoulder, then touched his stubbled cheek. "You know, you might turn out to be more than just a pretty face."

I whistled for Lucky.

"Goodbye, Michael."

"Goodbye, Eve."

Certain nothing I saw could turn me into a pillar of salt, I looked back just once. At the far end of the park, about to cross the street, I could just make out a tall man with a child on either side, a small hand held protectively in each of his own, too far away to hear a shout, never mind my whispered benediction.

"Michael, as a great poet once said… *Vaya con* fucking *Dios.*" I clapped my hands sharply. "C'mon Lucky! Where's Lisa? Go find her!"

Nearly dislocating the arm that held his leash, the big black dog dragged me, running and laughing, toward the girl in the distance who held an invisible string connected to a shining banner of rippling colours, floating a hundred feet high in the wind.

I've never come to like the Surrey Indoor Flea Market. It always reminds me too much of too many things in the past. But it's business and I settled into the routine, safe behind the table with Buzz or the other dealers. When I found myself looking up into the eyes of someone I knew, I had to think hard and fast to remember. He seemed to be trying to believe his eyes while I was trying to recall his name and where I knew him from.

"Eve…?"

A quarter dropped in the nearby machine that dispensed a handful of stale salted peanuts. It was Guy, Laine's young man before Mark, the one who'd run off with the stripper, who must be the bleached blonde with the poodle haircut standing beside him in an acid-wash denim ensemble, looking extravagantly bored and jealous on principle.

"What are you doing here?"

I smiled at him.

"I could ask you the same question."

"Oh, you know…Just going around the flea markets for a laugh." He flushed, afraid he might have offended me, and tried to change the subject. "Do you still see…?"

"No, I don't see anybody."

His companion interrupted us petulantly.

"Do we have to keep doing this? It's all just a bunch of old crap. Who cares about any of this shit? Let's *go* somewhere and *do* something…"

Guy picked up a gold bracelet from my table. It was one of the first things Michael had given me, one of the last souvenirs of that part of my life.

"This is a lovely piece. Just a sec, hon. This is nice work…"

I'd almost forgotten. So had he.

"Yes, it is, Guy. After all, you made it."

Hefting it in his hand, he looked at it like a man waking from a long drugged sleep.

"You're right... I did."

The girl threw it a grudging glance and popped her gum.

"It's okay, I guess."

I was tempted to tell Guy to take it back as a gift, to bring him luck. Then I thought about luck, what good it is and what people make of it, and gave him my best second-hand store smile.

"It's worth half a grand. I was asking three fifty. But for you, Guy, two ninety-five. If I skip lunch and bus home, I'll break even."